"You might not like riding wet."

Monty looked up at skies that had grown heavy with ponderous clouds. She swung her leg over the motorcycle seat and reached for his hand to steady herself.

"With you, Sebastian, I'm sure riding wet would be quite an adventure."

His eyes met hers like a flash fire; sexual awareness burned her senses and bled into her cheeks. She almost never blushed, and she wasn't easily embarrassed, but something about Sebastian was so...seductive. And she didn't even know if he meant to seduce her—or if he *wanted* to do so.

He kept her fingers enclosed within his gloved fist, and the touch of the leather against her skin felt deliciously sensual. When his lips formed a smoothly alluring curve, her heart did a dropkick and fluttered halfway between heaven and hell. She swallowed hard.

"I, uh, meant to say riding in the rain would be an adventure."

"I am your adventure, *mademoiselle*. Enjoy me, as I am enjoying you."

ABOUT THE AUTHOR

Karen Toller Whittenburg lives in the beautiful green country of northeastern Oklahoma. Her favorite pastime hasn't changed since she was a child—curling up with a good book. She divides her leisure time between a part-time job and family activities. She also scripts movies for the Narrative Television Network, a network for the blind and visually impaired. Karen and her husband love to spend weekends browsing through antique shops. He collects old cameras and she collects ideas for future books.

Books by Karen Toller Whittenburg

HARLEQUIN AMERICAN ROMANCE

197—SUMMER CHARADE
249—A MATCHED SET
294—PEPPERMINT KISSES
356—HAPPY MEDIUM
375—DAY DREAMER
400—A PERFECT PAIR
424—FOR THE FUN OF IT
475—BACHELOR FATHER
528—WEDDING OF HER DREAMS

HARLEQUIN TEMPTATION

303—ONLY YESTERDAY

Karen Toller Whittenburg

THE PAUPER AND THE PRINCESS

Harlequin Books

TORONTO • NEW YORK • LONDON
AMSTERDAM • PARIS • SYDNEY • HAMBURG
STOCKHOLM • ATHENS • TOKYO • MILAN
MADRID • WARSAW • BUDAPEST • AUCKLAND

ISBN 0-373-16552-8

THE PAUPER AND THE PRINCESS

Chapter One

The château could have sprung, tower to turret, hulking and whole, straight from a fairy tale. But if any princess had ever graced these halls, she had long since fallen under the sorcerer's spell, and like the château, could only dream of being awakened by a handsome—or more important, a very wealthy—prince.

The château's design was grandiose, the workmanship centuries old. History oozed from the mortar and dribbled across the coat of arms above the huge wooden door. Carved statues hunkered in alcoves four stories up, guardians, no doubt, of the vineyards in the valley below. Two circular towers bordered the north and south corners, ancient sentinels cast in deep shadow by angry, roiling clouds that obscured all but a glimmer of moonlight.

Beside the arched stone entrance, an electric torch flickered at erratic intervals, vying with the lightning that made an occasional stab across the night sky. An odor of neglect and disinterest seeped from beneath the great door to issue a musty welcome.

As if, Monty thought sarcastically, any self-respecting princess would ever set foot inside this Frankensteinesque castle. Reaching up, she grasped the cold brass ring of the knocker and slapped it against the doorplate. The sound echoed like a toothache inside the massive cavern on the other side of the door. Turning, Monty caught a glimpse of her companion and frowned. "For heaven's sake, Eve, quit gawking! It's only a castle. Anyone would think you're a tourist." She gave the brass knocker another impatient jolt. "Act as if you own the place."

"Yes, Miss Carlisle."

Monty wished she had an aspirin. "Let's go over this once more," she said. "While we're in France, we're going to pretend that you're me and I'm you. I'm Eve O'Halloran. You're Montgomery Carlisle. Remember. You're me. I'm you. Have we got that straight?"

"Yes, Miss Carlisle."

Monty never sighed and she wasn't about to start now... even though at the moment she had plenty of good reasons. "This is not a tough assignment, Eve, and you did agree with me that it might be kind of fun to exchange identities. So, when anyone addresses you as Monty or Mademoiselle Carlisle, give some indication that you recognize the name. That's it. The rest of the time, if you want, you can ignore everybody. One of the peculiarities of being an heiress is that no one really expects you to behave like a decent human being. So while we're here, you're getting paid to do whatever you like...*except* to call me Miss Carlisle—''

The huge door moaned like an out-of-tune cello and swung slowly inward. The musty odor rushed out to greet them, blending and then fading into the night air. A stout woman stood in the entry, a kerosene lantern held aloft in her hand, its flicker of light casting an eerie glow over the wild white cobweb that was her hair. Her eyes were dark slits above round rouged cheeks. She said nothing, just stood there staring at them. Except for the mad-scientist hairdo, Monty couldn't tell much difference between the woman and the statues on the wall above.

"Bonsoir," she said, mutilating the greeting so it sounded like it had been born in Texas and raised in Omaha. Then she pronounced each word slowly, in carefully modulated and precise English, to further the effect of an American who didn't know *bonjour* from *arrivederci.* "I am Eve O'Halloran and this is Miss Carlisle. We have traveled all day and are very tired. Could you show us to our rooms right away, plea—uh, *s'il vous plaît?"*

The woman didn't wince at Monty's atrocious accent. She just turned her dour look on Eve and held the lantern slightly higher as she stepped back. "This way," she said in a voice that was nearly as flat as Kansas and at least as American.

Monty nudged her secretary to move across the threshold and out of the wind that was whipping across the valley. "Are you from the States?" she asked the woman as she followed an awestruck Eve into the cavernous hall.

The question echoed like a pinball shot into the shadows. "My name is Charlotte," the woman announced, as if that were an explanation. "The electricity is out."

Which was not quite accurate. A few valiant bulbs in the trio of chandeliers that hung overhead offered a flickering and unpredictable illumination, contributing an eerie incandescence to the great hall. The scratchy sound of underfed filaments snapped and crackled in the cool air. Spotty patches of light came from sconces mounted on walls that seemed to extend endlessly into the otherwise immense blackness that comprised the castle interior. A row of windows on either side of the entry were draped and covered, preventing even the infrequent flashes of lightning from entering.

Monty figured the whole place would only look worse in daylight. "Is there something wrong with the generator?" she asked.

Charlotte gave a careless shrug. "What am I? An electrician? Come this way."

Monty gave up expecting her companion to take charge. Eve was standing, mouth open, staring at the sweeping staircase and the vast, dark ceiling overhead. While the overall effect was a little spooky, Monty saw no reason to gape. "Have someone bring our luggage in," she said to Charlotte. "We left everything outside."

"There's no one here." Charlotte swung the lantern in a wide arc as she led the way toward the staircase. "I'll show you upstairs to your rooms, but you'll have to carry the bags in yourself."

Monty had fallen into step behind Charlotte, but stopped in her tracks. "What do you mean, there's no one here? Where is the caretaker? I'm sure my man of affairs arranged for him to hire a full-service staff."

"There's no one here to fetch the bags," Charlotte reiterated. "You'll have to do it, yourself...after I've shown you where the bedrooms are."

"Wait just a minute. Are you saying that *you* are the entire service staff?"

"I didn't say that." Charlotte proceeded toward the stairway as if she expected to be followed. "What I said was, there's no one here to fetch your bags."

"B-b-but..." Eve's voice started, then stuttered into silence.

Monty couldn't—and didn't—believe Edwin would have sent her here without making the proper arrangements. "I want to know where the caretaker is. There's no excuse for this sort of inconvenience and I insist..." Monty paused, recalling that she was the secretary in this scenario. She tempered her tone of authority. "Miss Carlisle will be staying at the château for several weeks. See that a service staff is in place tomorrow morning."

"Perhaps, Miss Carlisle should have brought a staff with her...to avoid such inconvenience." The deep, rich and faintly foreign voice came out of the dark-

ness to the right, startling Monty and making Eve
jump like an alley cat caught between a snarling dog
and a six-foot fence.

"And who are you?" Monty squinted into the
murky gloom. "The resident ghost?"

Eve gasped at the idea and Monty shot her a buck-
up-or-else scowl.

"Not a ghost," the throaty voice assured. "Just a
simple gardener."

The man who stepped into the circle of lantern light
didn't look like a gardener, and as far as Monty could
see, there wasn't anything *simple* about him. Tall,
dark, aristocratic, he might have been a descendant of
royalty or the firstborn son of the devil. He was large,
his physical presence alone somehow consuming and
commanding his surroundings like a panther in the
night, all grace, cunning and waiting power. The
clothing he wore was dark and unremarkable, except
for the muscular body it covered. A body Monty sus-
pected didn't rely on weights and workout equipment
for its maintenance.

His hair was long, sweeping back from his high
forehead and falling in careful dishevelment to his
shoulders, framing his handsome face in a dark halo.
Even in the indistinct light, his eyes appeared midnight dark, compelling and infinitely mysterious. A
restive energy emanated from him and encircled
Monty in its fierce and confusing force.

As he moved closer, the air in her lungs rushed to
her throat, making breathing difficult and speaking

impossible. She, who hadn't been intimidated by man or beast since the age of ten, found herself reduced to silence while his disquieting gaze ran over her from head to foot. The way his lips curved in something less than a smile made her stomach flutter in a strange manner.

"Welcome, Mademoiselle Carlisle, to your château." He made a slight and courtly bow. "I am Sebastian, the gardener."

"I—I am M-Miss Carlisle," Eve announced in a wavery, uncertain voice. "This is my sec-secretary, Miss O'Halloran."

Sebastian quickly concealed his surprise, but not before Monty made note of it. She noticed, too, that when he turned from her to Eve, he did so with a trace of reluctance. He repeated the bow for Eve and flashed a devastating smile. "Please forgive my mistake, *mademoiselle*. We have heard stories of the American heiress...." He gave a disarming shrug. "I did not expect to find you so quiet and ... shy."

Eve lost what little courage she might have had, and Monty stepped forward to save her—and to get a closer look at that smile. "Miss Carlisle is tired. We've traveled all day and she needs to rest. It would be extremely helpful, Sebastian, if you would bring in our luggage while Charlotte shows us to our rooms."

For all her politeness, it was still an order, and Monty waited for his reaction. His eyes met hers, introducing a challenge, revealing a flare of resentment and changing the flutter in her stomach into a knot of excitement. She didn't want to be in this musty old castle in the Loire Valley, and she'd been dreading the days ahead with every vibrant cell of her body. But suddenly her enforced exile from civilization held at least one intriguing possibility. "You don't mind fetching our bags, do you, Sebastian?"

"It will be my pleasure to retrieve your luggage, *mademoiselle.*" His smile mocked her as he dazzled Eve with it once again. "And those of your secretary, too, of course."

"Thank you." Eve nodded, even though she kept looking nervously at the darkness around them. "I don't think I could manage my own bags, much less Miss—"

Monty coughed, deep and loudly, then cleared her throat until it protested with pain. "I hope I'm not catching a chill. This is a drafty old place, isn't it? Did you say you were the gardener, Sebastian?"

"Oui, mademoiselle." He dipped his head in a manner that was anything but subservient. "I have just only begun to restore the gardens," he said. "But it would be an honor to escort Mademoiselle Carlisle...and you, too, of course, about the grounds. Tomorrow if you like."

Monty met his eyes...and a confusing awareness blended with a sudden skepticism. She turned to Eve, but kept her gaze fixed on Sebastian. "Isn't it odd that a gardener has been hired to restore the gardens, when there is only Charlotte to staff the château, itself?"

"Nothing odd about it." Charlotte's mid-American twang sounded out of place in the great, dark hall. "No one wants to work here. The place is haunted."

"H-h-haunted?" Eve's eyes got that wide, panicked look again. "What do you mean, *haunted?*"

Charlotte frowned. "You know. Ghosts and goblins and things that go bump in the night. *Haunted.*"

Monty laughed. "Do you tell that story to every visitor, Charlotte? Or only on dark, stormy nights when the electricity is out?"

Charlotte lifted the lantern, framing her stern expression in an unearthly light. "We don't get many visitors. You can believe what you want, but don't come crying to me when you run into one of the ghosts that walks these halls."

"I don't suppose any of them could be trained as service staff, could they?" Monty wasn't surprised that Charlotte didn't see the humor, but Sebastian's rich chuckle sent a warm feeling all through her.

"You will have to catch one first," he said.

"Maybe I already have. You don't look like a gardener, Sebastian."

"And you, *mademoiselle,* do not look like a secretary."

"Tomorrow I'll wear a typewriter around my neck."

"And I shall wear overalls and a straw hat."

Touché. By sheer force of will, she turned from his mesmerizing dark eyes to face the stoic and lantern-lit Charlotte. "What about the caretaker? Where is he?"

"Louis?"

For the first time since their arrival, Monty thought Charlotte seemed rattled. The glance the woman exchanged with Sebastian confirmed the suspicion, and his quick answer cinched it. "Louis is away. On business."

"Rather poor timing on his part, isn't it?"

"A coincidence, nothing more." Charlotte turned again to the stairway. "I'll show you where you'll be sleeping for the night."

"We'll be staying a bit longer than one night."

Charlotte looked over her shoulder, and in the eerie light her pale eyes flashed with hidden meaning. "Of course, you will," she said. "This way."

"W-w-wait." Eve touched trembling fingers to her lips. "Are w-w-we all alone in this . . . this p-place?"

"That depends on what you mean by alone." Charlotte took obvious pleasure in her evasive answer, and Eve, just as obviously, found no comfort in it. "Besides," the older woman continued, "we were told you wanted solitude, Miss Carlisle. Complete and uninterrupted solitude."

Eve turned to Monty, clearly intimidated, and said in a low voice, "I don't think I want to do this."

Monty swept the back of her hand across her forehead, pushing aside the chestnut hair that swung forward at the side of her face. She was tired, she realized. Probably due more to the previous week's round of parties commemorating her banishment than to the trans-Atlantic flight. Jet lag had its drawbacks, but it couldn't hold a candle to a well-rooted hangover. "We'll be fine," she assured her secretary before turning a question to Sebastian. "I assume there are proper security measures in place?"

"Oh, don't worry. Seb will protect you." Charlotte and the lantern light bobbed under an archway and up the wide staircase.

Monty looked at Sebastian, trying unsuccessfully to read his expression before the shadows closed in around him.

"There is no need for alarm, *mademoiselle*. Everything is in place." With another slight bow, he walked to the door, the heels of his boots clicking brusquely against the stone floor. The door creaked as he pulled it open, admitting the sounds and scent of falling rain. A streak of lightning pierced the sky, brightening the entry for a split second and turning Sebastian into a tall, dark silhouette. Then he was gone and the door swung closed with a groan.

Monty turned to follow Charlotte up the stairs, but Eve grabbed her arm. "What did she mean, 'Seb will protect us'? Protect us from what? The ghosts?"

"You're beginning to sound like Aunt Josephine." Monty freed herself from Eve's death grip and lowered her voice. "If you'll recall, I came here to get away from all that nonsense. There is nothing to be afraid of. No ghosts. No wicked stepmothers. No evil fairy intent on luring Sleeping Beauty into the turret. Didn't I warn you that Aunt Jo was full of crazy superstitions and ridiculous fairy tales and that you shouldn't listen to a word she says?"

"B-b-but this place is so creepy."

"I'm sure it looks quite homey in the daylight. Use your imagination," Monty said firmly.

Eve sighed as she twisted her hands in a nervous clasp. "You're right. This is supposed to be your holiday and I'm spoiling it for you."

"This is not my idea of a holiday, and I don't think there's a thing you could do that would make it any worse." She squinted through the archway at the shadowy staircase. "Now, where did that woman go?"

"I don't know, but I'd feel a lot safer if I were carrying the lantern."

Monty placed her hand at Eve's back and urged her up the stairs in Charlotte's wake, but it was like trying to push a mule. Every other step, Eve balked. "I can barely see the stairs."

"Sit down, then. I'll go get the lantern and come back for you."

Eve looked alarmed. "Oh, I can't let you do that. You might get hurt."

"I'm not going to spend the night on these stairs, I can tell you that." She looked up at the winding darkness. "Charlotte!"

Like magic, the lantern light illuminated the top of the stairwell and Charlotte's voice boomed down. "This way."

Monty frowned at the abrupt command, but the light was already moving on and away. "Come on, Eve. We'll get that lantern one way or another." She sprinted up the remaining steps and heard Eve's faltering steps behind her. But when she reached the top of the stairs, she discovered Charlotte was little more than a slight glow far down the hall.

"Charlotte," Monty called, the name bouncing down the hallway like a rubber ball. "Charlotte!"

"This way." Coarse and impatient, Charlotte's voice echoed back from the dark cave on the left. The circlet of light bobbed up, down and then out of sight.

Eve's hand closed over Monty's forearm. "It's so dark up here," she whispered. "Where did she go?"

"Maybe the bedrooms open off this hallway." Monty strained to catch a second glimpse of the lantern. A flash of lightning streaked the night sky outside the second-floor windows, illuminating the long hallway and the angelic statues that stood guard along the corridor. Darkness prevailed again, but Monty moved forward with renewed purpose, pulling Eve along with her.

"I can't see a thing," Eve whispered hoarsely. "Don't you think we should wait for her to come back for us? We don't know where we're going. We don't even know where we are."

"We're in the hall of angels."

"Angels? Are you sure?"

Monty peered into an alcove, her eyes struggling to identify the outline of a doorway that might substantiate her theory that the bedrooms were located nearby. "Well, I suppose the statues could be saints, but I think I can make out wings...yes, those are definitely angels.''

A noise rippled around them—a rumbling, low and distant and familiar. Monty jumped, startled by the sound, apprehensive in the darkness and unsettled by her own wavering fortitude.

"Wh-wh-what was that?" Eve stood very still, listening.

"Thunder."

"It didn't sound like thunder."

Monty frowned, impatient with the whole world and in particular, with Charlotte. "I suppose it could have been Sebastian dragging our suitcases across the drawbridge and dropping them into the moat."

"There isn't a drawbridge...or a moat."

Monty continued to move slowly down the hallway, distracted and searching for the lantern light. Pausing under the outspread wings of one of the statues, she raised her voice. "Charlotte? We need the lantern out here."

"Charlotte?" Eve repeated the name in a voice as insubstantial as a feather. "Charlotte?"

"This way." The voice echoed from the darkness three angels down. The lantern flashed a signal, then vanished again.

"Oh, there she is." Relief rushed out of Eve on a heavy sigh, and she moved quickly toward the light. "This way."

"This way," Monty mimicked under her breath. Edwin had better have a damn good explanation for not telling her to pack a flashlight.

Outside, a shower of raindrops pelted the window-panes. Monty paused to look out at the storm, thinking that she wouldn't even be here if it hadn't been for Edwin and that unfortunate business about the ruby....

A lightning bolt zigzagged across the sky, accompanied by a crash of thunder. The back of her neck prickled and all around her the night became electric, giving a split-second warning, offering her a fateful moment to react. She turned, aware of a scraping noise, conscious of danger but suspended in a breathless limbo, as the angel above her rocked on its base, tipped and...

A grip as strong as steel jerked her off her feet and out of the path of the statue as it plunged to the floor. The arms of her savior held her securely against a wall of muscled power, a wall that moved in and out in a series of short, ragged breaths—breaths that matched the frightened rhythm of her own. Behind her head, she felt dampness and then the pulsing beat of his heart. In her throat, her own heart was beating like that of a trapped bird. The smell of storm and rain surrounded her rescuer and saturated every ragged breath she drew. His strength supported her, and the vagrant thought slipped through her mind that her grip on his forearms had to hurt. But she couldn't let go, couldn't find her voice to thank him, couldn't look away from the fallen angel at her feet.

Down the hall, Eve's cry of alarm was cut short by Charlotte's stern and very American, "What the hell was that?"

An instant later, Eve was beside her, and the strong arms that had held Monty were gone... vanished like a trail of smoke in the wind. Her hands had nothing to hold except empty air, and she trembled in the sudden cold.

Charlotte grumbled as she reached the scene and held up the lantern, moving the light across the broken statue. "Now, how did you manage to do that?"

"Oh, no." Eve's whispered horror ran through Monty like the chill of a fever, and she longed for the healing embrace of her rescuer. "You might have been killed. Oh, I knew we shouldn't have come to this place. I was afraid something would happen. It's the curse, isn't it?"

The Carlisle Curse... The Last Heir... Memory echoed Aunt Josephine's oft-repeated warnings through Monty's brain. *Will Die... Will Die... Will Die...*

"Nonsense," she said, grabbing the tail of logic and giving it a shake. "I wasn't in any danger. I must have bumped against the pedestal and knocked the thing over. If you hadn't left us in the dark, Charlotte, this wouldn't have happened."

"Well, it isn't my fault." The woman shrugged. "I thought you were behind me."

Below in the great hall, the heavy front door squawked as it was pushed open. The faint sound of rain preceded a rush of storm-scented air up through the chasms of the great room below and into the hall of the angels. A suitcase hit the floor with a dull thud, followed by the complaint of the door as it was closed. Heavy footsteps moved in the hall, stopped, then moved again. Sebastian began to whistle as he started up the stairs.

Monty caught her breath. But it couldn't be Sebastian. He had just pulled her from danger, held her, protected her. Her body still retained a degree of his warmth. The back of her blouse had absorbed a slight dampness from his shirt and was now a cool reminder of his presence. Her heart was still pounding with the feel of his arms around her. Her pulse was racing with the knowledge that he hadn't simply held her, he had held her close . . . as a lover might have done. Sebastian was her rescuer. She was sure of it. But when he crested the stairs, a suitcase under each arm and one in each hand, the certainty slipped away.

"You didn't have to wait for me," he said easily, his breathing quick but not noticeably labored. "I was planning to bring the bags directly to the bedrooms." He took one look at Eve's pale face and set down the luggage. "Is something wrong?"

"An a-a-accident," Eve replied.

Charlotte jerked her head in Monty's direction, demonstrating her opinion with a loud sniff. "*She* bumped the statue and knocked it off."

Seb approached and knelt, touching the angel with a light, inquisitive hand. He stood and transferred his interest to the pedestal, running his hand over the flat marble surface. Only then did he allow his gaze to wander to Monty's flushed face. "Were you hurt?"

Monty realized she'd been holding her breath, awaiting the visual contact that now seared her skin with heated awareness. He knew she was all right. He had been there to save her. Otherwise, he would have turned first to her and then to the statue. "I'm fine," she said in a voice that sounded too hollow to belong to her. "I wasn't hurt at all. My guardian angel must have been close by."

Even in the dim light, she could see the tightening of his lips, and the mystery knotted inside her. "You are fortunate, Mademoiselle O'Halloran. You could have been injured."

"I'm fine," she repeated, consciously inhaling deep, slow breaths. "It was just an accident."

"Did it scare you?"

Her heart skipped a beat. "Was it supposed to?"

As an answer, his smile was cryptic, but Monty felt its potency all the way to her fingertips. With a shrug, he turned to retrieve the bags. "As you say, it was an accident."

Of course it had been an accident. No one else had been anywhere near the statue. No one except her... and the man who had saved her.

She reached for the lantern with fingers suddenly gone numb. "Let me carry that. Miss Carlisle can't keep up with you."

There was resistance, but Monty was in no mood to argue. Charlotte frowned and let go of the lantern. Monty held it up, deliberating spilling the light away from Sebastian. She couldn't look at him now, couldn't face the questions whirling through her thoughts, couldn't even imagine the answers. She turned her challenge to Charlotte. "This way?"

The woman nodded curtly and moved down the hall. "Stay with me this time. There are three more sets of stairs before we reach the bedrooms, so keep up."

With a last frightened glance at the fallen angel, Eve scurried after Charlotte's formidable figure. Monty turned, keeping the light directed on the hallway ahead, waiting pointedly for Sebastian to move past.

He remained in the shadows. "I will follow behind you, *mademoiselle,* and protect you from the angels."

Monty fought the tiny thrill that gathered at her nape and rippled down her spine. A thrill that was equal parts fear, exhilaration and fantasy. In this one brief evening, in this dark, deserted château, she had encountered a ghost, a gardener and a guardian angel.

And somehow they were all named Sebastian.

Chapter Two

Trouble had arrived.

Seb shifted the weight of the luggage he carried as he followed the glow of the lantern and the sassy sway of Eve O'Halloran's hips into one of the château's sixteen bedchambers. Like gray hovering ghosts, four shadows crept over the tapestry-covered walls and stretched upward to encroach upon the high ceiling. The huge four-poster bed seemed small and forlorn in the oversize room and the other pieces of furniture were few and scattered about, arranged to disguise the fact that so many were missing. The room smelled of disuse and disinfectant. And now, it was being invaded by the scent of a woman.

Trouble, he thought. At the worst possible time. And of the worst possible kind.

"You'll sleep in here, Miss Carlisle." Charlotte gestured at the bed. "And your secretary in there." She pointed at a door almost completely concealed in the wall. "The rooms adjoin."

"It's so... large."

Seb assessed the American heiress from the corner of his eye. She was pale, almost ethereal in the darkness, and he wondered if she would fade into her surroundings in the sunlight. Her eyes were big and blue, her hair a nondescript brown, and she was pretty enough, he supposed. Prettier actually than her secretary... if one preferred pearls over rubies, Monet over van Gogh. Mademoiselle O'Halloran was a vivid contrast to her employer, a splash of color in the dark, a dab of bright paint streaking a black canvas with life. And she was trouble.

She placed the lantern on an ornate table, and Seb watched with interest as she quickly took in the details of the room. "It isn't exactly the Ritz, is it?"

He hid his smile. So, the little secretary preferred the lap of luxury. That, at least, he might be able to turn to his advantage.

"Where should I place your bags, Mademoiselle Carlisle?" he asked the heiress.

"Oh, anywhere, thank you." Her voice was tiny, just shy of a whisper, and she stared at the bedroom as if it might suddenly come alive and gobble her up.

"Put those two by the armoire." Mademoiselle O'Halloran pointed out the division of bags with an air of authority. "And bring the rest in here."

She had opened the adjoining door and was exploring the room beyond without the lantern, with only the gray light of the rainy night outside to guide her. By the time Seb entered the room, she had opened one pair of the floor-length windows and was standing in the opening. The wind whipped across the balcony to catch the ends of her shoulder-length hair and toss it like so much chaff. She stretched her arms to take in the storm and lifted her face to the moisture that penetrated the night. And she laughed, a soft, throaty murmur of pleasure that curled through the darkness to wrap around him like a cat purring at his feet.

Seb realized he was staring and moved to set down her bags. As he walked up behind her, the tantalizing fragrance that surrounded her blended with the smell of the rain in the gardens below to fill his senses with a sharp and vivid memory. The impulse to take hold of her shoulders and pull her back against his body was sudden, powerful and annoying. He stepped around her and closed the windows with crisp efficiency. "It's best to keep the moisture out, *mademoiselle.*"

She looked at him, and he was struck by the spark of challenge in her deep blue eyes. "I beg your pardon?" she said.

"It's raining." He indicated the weather with a flowing gesture, as if she had somehow forgotten the storm. "Outside, the rain nurtures. Inside, it can cause untold damage."

"Thank you for that insight, Mr. Science." She reached for the window latch. "But I believe everyone and everything needs fresh air."

The windows opened again, freed by her touch, and Seb tamped down his irritation. This château had been built centuries ago, had withstood the destructive forces of war and revolution and human foible. And she, on some irrational whim, chose to expose it to the elements that could insidiously destroy it. *"Mademoiselle,"* he said tightly. "You complained earlier of feeling chilled. Please allow me to close the windows."

She barely turned her head in his direction. "I'm feeling fine now, thanks. My brush with the angel seems to have warmed me considerably."

A swirl of mixed emotions raced through him, causing a tingling sensation in his fingertips, making him want to bury his hands in the luxuriant fire of her hair, place his thumbs on the hollow of her throat. He clenched his fists at his sides and managed a slight bow. "It might easily have been the angel of death, *mademoiselle.*"

She stiffened. "It was an accident. Nothing more."

"Yes, of course."

She looked at him then, and he saw the first flicker of uncertainty defy the confidence in her eyes. "Are you trying to frighten me, Sebastian?"

He shrugged, pleased that he had ruffled her. "I am merely trying to close the windows. You could be exposing yourself to . . . unnecessary danger."

"Really?" Her chin lifted and the trace of vulnerability in her eyes disappeared. "Well, I appreciate your concern. You may leave now."

Her haughty tone fueled the urge to grab her, to shake her, to hold her. . . .

"Don't you need some light in here?"

Seb turned to the open doorway, where Montgomery Carlisle hovered like a timid deer. She held a pair of silver candlesticks, complete with lighted candles, and in their wavery glow she appeared just this side of terrified. "Oh, please, don't stand in the window like that," she said in a rush of anxiety. "You could catch pneumonia or...or something awful could happen. You could fall to your death from this height."

Seb pressed the point. "I was just giving your secretary the same advice, Mademoiselle Carlisle, but she seems impervious to our opinions."

"Yes, she is often immune to common sense."

"*And* unreasonable fears." Monty gave Eve a small frown and was glad to see the candles in her hand quiver. "I see you found some light to brighten this place."

Eve turned to shield the flames with her body. "Charlotte found these candles," she said. "If you don't mind, I thought I would keep the lantern in my room and you could keep the candles in here...but I'm afraid they won't be much use, with all the wind and rain coming through that window."

Monty didn't care where the candles were placed, but she was tired of this argument, and with a toss of her head in Seb's general direction, she made a production out of closing the windows. "There," she said. "Now you both can sleep comfortably, knowing I'm safe from chills and whatever dangers lurk in this gloomy old castle." An interesting idea crossed her mind, and she turned to Sebastian. "Does the château have a dungeon? Are there any secret passage-ways?"

"You have been reading fairy tales, *mademoiselle.*" He smiled, a genuine smile, and Monty felt the response kick her in the backs of her knees. "No doubt the château has many secrets," he continued, "but I am familiar only with those in the gardens."

"That's right. You are just a simple gardener, aren't you, Sebastian?"

He made a slight bow, but his eyes held fast to hers, issuing a challenge she was pleased to see and determined to meet.

"Your bed is ready, Miss Carlisle," Charlotte announced as she passed Eve and entered the room. With hands on hips, she frowned at Monty. "Can you turn down your own covers or do you want me to do it?"

Service with a smile apparently wasn't one of the amenities at *le château Carlisle,* Monty thought. "As long as the sheets have been changed at least once in the past four hundred years, I can manage, thank you."

Charlotte might have been offended, but her expression was too close to call. "There's fresh linen in the cupboard if the ones on the bed don't suit you." She turned and bypassed Eve once again, not bothering to say goodbye, good-night, or even the good old standard "sleep tight, don't let the bedbugs bite."

Seb moved to follow her, but stopped beside Eve, who, in the flickering light of the candles, looked as if she had been dropped smack into the pages of *Jane Eyre.*

"Mademoiselle Carlisle?" he said gently. "May I take the candlesticks for you?"

"Oh, yes, please." She handed them over eagerly, and in his hands the flames immediately grew brighter. "Do you think the electricity will be back on by tomorrow night, Sebastian?"

"Of course, it will," Monty said as she stepped into the candlelight's golden circle. "This isn't the Dark Ages. You'll have the generator running first thing in the morning, won't you, Sebastian?"

He turned to her and, again, an energizing spark passed between them, making Monty completely and only aware of the mysterious man who faced her. The silence crackled around her for the space of a heartbeat...or perhaps longer. "It will be my pleasure to do what I can to make Mademoiselle Carlisle happy."

No small task, Monty thought, but she gave him one of her most encouraging smiles, anyway. "That's good to know, Sebastian."

He answered with another bow and then turned away, but not before Monty saw the long strand of chestnut-colored hair which lay caught in the fabric of his shirt. A strand of *her* hair. Her heart jumped to her throat. Her eyes flew to question his, but he was already moving toward the bed, carrying the candlesticks to a marble-topped table.

It had been Sebastian who had rescued her, had held her in his arms, had infused her with his body heat and a heady desire. And it had been Sebastian who had entered the château through the front door a scant few minutes later. The discovery created confusion and an agitation born of an unknown fear.

"Thank you, Sebastian." Eve moved closer to the bed, the light and the gardener. "You've been so very helpful."

"Good night, *mademoiselle*." He walked to the doorway and paused beside Monty, who watched him now with new interest. His gaze was a caress that made her shiver. "Sleep well."

She reached out and lifted the strand of hair from his shirt, drawing it carefully through her fingers, taking care to hold it so he could see. "I don't think the ghosts will bother me tonight. I have a guardian angel, you know."

He looked at the evidence and didn't blink. "Be careful, *mademoiselle*. Angels have been known to fall from grace." With a nod, he walked from the room. His footsteps echoed hollowly as he crossed the first bedchamber, and then there was a soft thud as he closed the door behind him. An eerie silence bubbled like a witch's brew.

Eve shivered and hugged herself. "This is like a gigantic spook house. Aren't you cold?"

Monty drew the strand of hair through her fingertips again, thoughtfully considering its implications. "Our welcome has been on the chilly side, hasn't it? I'll phone Uncle Edwin tomorrow and find out what arrangements were made and why the caretaker isn't here. That seems very odd.''

"It all seems odd to me.'' Eve began to wring her hands. "Couldn't we just get back in the car and return to Paris?''

"Are you kidding? Wild horses couldn't drag me away from here tonight. For one thing, I'm too tired to get back into that ridiculous little car Edwin rented for us. And for another, I believe a little investigative work is called for. Something very strange is going on.''

"Well, then, would you fire me now? I'm too responsible to quit and leave you alone in this…this…''

"*This* is Château Carlisle.'' Monty looked around the room, watched the shadows created by the dancing candle flames and wondered if a ghost could have eyes as dark as a Mediterranean night. "And for the first time since I heard the name, I think I'm going to like it here.''

MONTY AWAKENED WITH a start, her heart pounding, her eyes seeking substance, her mind grasping for reality in the unfamiliar darkness. The château. The electricity was out. She turned her head toward the table. Yes, the candles were there, just as Sebastian had left them, although the flames had long since been extinguished. Eve was in the room next door, probably sleeping like a baby, despite her jittery nerves. Monty took a deep breath as she lay back on the pillow. She must have been dreaming, or rather having a nightmare. Considering the strange welcome she'd received, that was hardly surprising.

The storm had passed and moonlight curled through the windowpanes to litter the floor in silver ribbons. Monty yawned and rolled onto her side, thinking about the crisp, fresh feel of the sheets against her skin. Charlotte had prepared this room for guests. Obviously, Edwin had informed someone at the château of her arrival. Charlotte hadn't just dropped in out of the blue. So why did she have the feeling that she wasn't welcome here? Why did the thought keep recurring that perhaps the angel hadn't fallen by accident?

She'd fallen asleep thinking about that... and trying not to think about Sebastian de Vergille.

"Dangereuse."

Like the echo of a whisper, the word dropped into her consciousness—real, but not real; a sound she heard, but might just as easily have imagined. But since when did her imagination talk to her in French?

Monty pushed back the bed covers and swung her feet over the side of the mattress, scaring herself a little as she dropped the considerable distance to the floor. That first step was a dilly. A person could break a leg just getting out of bed.

Maybe she'd ask Seb to bring up a stepladder. No, not a good idea. As Montgomery Carlisle, she wouldn't hesitate to do that, but if she wanted to continue her masquerade as a meek and mild secretary for the duration of her exile, she should probably curtail such trivial demands.

"Dangereuse."

Halfway to the windows, Monty froze in her tracks. She hadn't imagined that soft, floating whisper. It came from somewhere nearby, a ghostly warning. *Dangerous.* Was it a signal? A harbinger of the Carlisle curse?

Monty straightened with a snap. Shades of Aunt Josephine, she thought. A few hours in this castle of horrors, mixed in with the foolish fables she'd been told since childhood, and she was a basket case. Standing barefoot in the middle of a stone cold bedchamber, straining to hear what she wasn't sure she'd heard in the first place.

Spinning on her heels she scurried back to the bed. She contemplated the leap required to make it up and onto the mattress, then turned around to face the windows. If she had heard a voice, it could have come from somewhere outside. She squared her shoulders and marched briskly and bravely to the windows. Grasping the latch, she pulled down and back and the windows sprang open, pouring cool, damp air into the room, touching her with a phantom chill. Monty shivered, told herself to buck up, then stood very still in the opening, listening for the whisper, waiting for that unearthly voice to speak again.

She heard it. A distant and deep growling that rose and fell like the nuances of conversation. A question, an answer, a comment, a reply. Yes, she decided. It was a conversation, but distinguishing the content was beyond her range of hearing. It was too far away, distorted, and seemed to have no direction. Monty moved onto the balcony, her bare feet making a quiet splash in the shallow puddles of rain left by the storm, the dampness seeping into her like icy morning dew. She placed her hands on the cold stone banister and looked down at the dark gardens below.

A cloud crossed the moon and the shadows shifted, moving like scattered dreams through the night. The faraway sounds disappeared, replaced by the scampering noises of insects and animals that stirred before dawn. There was thunder, too, as distant as the memory of the storm that now cluttered the horizon. Stars overhead blinked like the eyes of a child with wet, spiky eyelashes.

Monty leaned against the banister, trying to make something out of the nothingness and getting nothing but wet and cold for her trouble. She frowned, pushed back from the balcony rail . . . and saw him.

Sebastian.

His hair, his clothes blended into the darkness as if he were an inseparable part of the night. His face was the only feature she could see, a ghostly image in the center of the garden, watching her as she was watching him.

She had no idea how long she stood there, mesmerized by his gaze, with no sense of the wind whipping her hair into a fiery halo around her head, no recognition that her fingers and toes were growing numb with cold. When he turned his face away from her and dissolved into the darkness she was left with the awareness that something strange had happened, something elemental and basic, and totally beyond her range of experience.

Whatever it was, he controlled it. He moved through the darkness like a phantom, beside her in the hallway one minute, coming through the front door with her luggage the next. In the garden and then...gone. She didn't believe in ghosts, although she did know a few people who were among the walking dead. But this was different. Sebastian was real. Too warm, too strong, too male to inhabit any world but this one. So somewhere out there in the dark, there was a reasonable explanation. A way for him to be in two places at once.

And now, like Juliet, she stood on a balcony, seeking another glimpse of him, her heart pounding with the awareness that he had claimed her somehow, in those brief moments. She didn't understand how or why or what it meant, but she knew that she should get as far as possible from Sebastian de Vergille. He was a threat to her. He was *dangereux*.

A second shiver trickled down her spine, but it wasn't fear that flowed over her like warm honey. It was loneliness, pure and sweet and painful.

"IT'S TOO DANGEROUS. Louis should be here."

Seb shrugged aside Charlotte's concern and hefted the coil of rope onto his shoulder. "Louis has been gone for three days. We have no way of knowing when he will return. I can't afford to wait." He snapped a D-ring onto his belt and tightened the strap of his climbing gear. "Especially now that *she* is here."

"We can get rid of her. She's frightened already. With a little encouragement, she'll be gone tomorrow."

"I wish I felt so certain."

"Trust me. She's spoiled, thinking she can snap her fingers and have everything done. She's in for a rude awakening, if she thinks I'll scratch every time she has an itch."

Seb smiled. "I think she expected something more luxurious, perhaps. At least more comfortable. And I got the impression that our heiress isn't nearly as spoiled as her secretary would like to be."

"Miss O'Halloran will be a problem."

Seb averted his eyes and made another needless check of his gear. Charlotte was too perceptive at times, and he did not want her to know just how big a problem he believed Miss O'Halloran already was. "I'll figure out some way to get around her."

"Get on top of her, you mean. I saw the look you gave her."

"She's attractive," he said with an understated shrug. "And if romancing her is the way to find what I seek, then I will seduce her with my charm."

"Charm," Charlotte scoffed. "That one is trouble, Seb. Stay out of her bed."

"Would you prefer I romance the little heiress?"

"You have more to gain by making her fall in love with you. Think, Sebastian, the château could be yours." She snapped her fingers. "Just like that."

If only life were so simple, he thought. "I want only what is rightfully mine." He looked up at the sheer, steep wall of the south turret. "All I have to do is find it."

"But it's madness to climb the wall in this darkness."

"Would you have me do it in daylight?"

"It would be madness then, too. Wait until you can get into the tower through the passageway."

"The entrance off the tunnel is locked fast, and the outside door is sealed shut. I've been unable to find another way inside. Now that Mademoiselle Carlisle is here, I may not have any more opportunities to explore the passageways and this may be my only chance to attempt a climb."

Charlotte nervously fingered her apron sash. "But the windows in the tower are too small. You'll never fit through them, even if you manage the climb to the tower without breaking your foolish neck. It's dangerous."

Seb reached out to squeeze her hand. "Don't worry. I'll be in and out of the turret before sunrise, with no one the wiser. And I won't break my neck."

"I wish you didn't always do things the hard way, Seb. We'll get rid of the women. They won't last two days, without a bunch of stiff and starched servants. My cooking will be the final straw."

Seb laughed softly. "*Mademoiselle* will have a chef from Paris here within hours of tasting your fish stew."

"I'll leave the heads on the fish. That ought to put the squeeze on her pampered palate." Charlotte mulled that idea for a moment. "We'll think of something. And if all else fails, there may have to be another... accident."

Accident. The word brought on a memory, sharp and haunting, of the woman he had held in his arms, trembling within his embrace, her body curving into his, the fragrance of her hair in his nostrils, the thick texture of it against his jaw. She had been frightened, no matter what she said. But he didn't believe she would leave the château. Not until she had managed to interfere with all his careful plans.

He looked up at the château tower, all wet and slick from the rain, and he thought... of her. As he'd seen her on the balcony. With her hair tossed by the wind, the white nightdress pressed like a lover's hands against her body. He shouldn't have let her see him there in the garden, should have vanished the moment she stepped out of her bedroom. But she had held him bewitched, and then, of course, it had been too late.

Oh, yes. She was trouble. "*Dangereuse,*" he whispered.

And Charlotte, looking up at the dark tower, whispered her agreement. "*Dangereux.*"

Chapter Three

As expected, daylight did little to improve the château's appearance. With arms looped across her upraised knees, Monty sat in the center of the mammoth four-poster bed in the center of the massive high-ceilinged room, and wondered what madness had possessed her ancestor when he bought this medieval monstrosity.

Aunt Josephine had explained it with yet another family legend from her seemingly inexhaustible supply. They were all fairy tales in Monty's opinion, and she'd never paid them the least bit of attention. Now, however, she couldn't help wondering if there might be any truth to the story that Josiah Carlisle had been betrayed by a woman and had acquired the castle as a means of revenge.

Some revenge. Whatever French aristocrat had palmed off this place on old Josiah had certainly had the last laugh. Buying a French château wasn't the worst investment a Carlisle had ever made, but it hardly ranked up there as one of the great buys of the

century, either. If the truth were known, the Frenchman was probably still around, a cheerful ghost chor-
tling his way through eternity, forever amused by the
way he had bested the American industrialist.

Monty flung back the heavy bed covers and crawled
to the edge of the lumpy mattress, taking care as she
slid from the bed to the floor. Standing there, her bare
toes curled into the worn and ancient nap of a woven
rug, she studied the carved beams and cross beams
that comprised the ceiling. Dust and dirt had dulled
the patina and darkened the once rich paintings until
they were little more than a variation in the color of
the wood.

From one of the faded tapestries on the wall, Joan
of Arc sought guidance from above as she stood in the
midst of a battle scene. Monty squinted at the weav-
ing, but couldn't find a trace of a ruby pendant anywhere on Saint Joan, even though according to Aunt
Josephine's legend of the ruby, the lady never went
anywhere without it.

"You know, Joan," Monty said aloud. "If I were
a suspicious woman, I'd think Aunt Josephine had
arranged for you and I to share this room."

Joan made no comment on that theory.

"Well, you can believe what you want," Monty
said. "But if I'd thought the Carlisle Ruby actually
was once your talisman, I'd never have wagered it in
that silly bet with Stanton Grainger." She yawned in
the continuing silence, then lifted her shoulder in a

shrug. "All right, so I would have made the bet anyway, but it was nothing personal."

Another yawn sent her arms reaching for the ceiling, an unachievable aim even if she'd had a ladder. Bracing her arms against the dark, scrolled wood of the nearest bedpost, she did a couple of lazy exercises and decided that the room needed fresh air almost as badly as she did.

Dust motes scrambled for cover as she opened the windows to admit the sunbeams, which were pressed against the dirty panes like eager children outside a baker's shop. The air was glorious and Monty stepped out onto the small balcony, stretching her arms high above her head and breathing deeply of the rain-cleansed morning. A puff of a breeze scooted past, ruffling her hair and bringing with it the sound of Sebastian whistling a vaguely familiar melody.

A tingle of anticipation caused her heart to skip a beat, and Monty leaned over the stone banister to look for him in the tangle of overgrown gardens below. He had been easier to see in the dark, she decided, and she was a little surprised at the thrill that raced through her with the memory and the possibility of seeing him again.

"Miss Carlisle?" Eve's whisper followed her faint knock on the connecting door. "Miss Carli—?"

Monty cautioned her secretary with a wave of her hand and then wiggled farther out over the railing for a better vantage point.

"Oh, do be careful." Eve hovered in the window frame, her alarm a palpable thing. "P-p-please don't fall, Miss Carlisle."

"*Don't* call me that," Monty said over her shoulder. "And I'm not going to fall. This railing is wide enough to handle a team of Chinese acrobats."

"It looks very dangerous."

Monty wondered if her secretary had been dropped off a ledge as a child. That certainly would explain this unhealthy fear of balconies. "Well, it isn't. I'm only spying on our gorgeous gardener."

Eve stood on tiptoe and tried to see over the balcony rail without coming any closer to the edge. "Is he in the garden?"

"He was." The whistling had stopped, and she still hadn't caught a glimpse of the mysterious Sebastian. Disappointed, Monty straightened and turned her back on the gardens, bracing her hands behind her on the stone banister. "Did you have a restful night?"

Eve's shoulders sagged. "I didn't sleep a wink, did you?"

"I slept a thousand winks. Maybe a hundred thousand." Monty allowed herself a feel-good laugh. "Despite a valiant attempt by that mattress to toss me out of bed."

Eve looked at the four-poster. "I've never seen such beds. Or such a place. Are you certain you want to stay here?"

"*Au contraire, mademoiselle.* I'm quite certain this is the last place I want to be. But you know my Uncle

Edwin. He was livid over that silly business about the Carlisle Ruby and insisted that I hide out somewhere until he's taken care of the problem. And every time he mentioned that I'd be lucky if Stanton Grainger didn't hire a hit man, Aunt Josephine would go into hysterics and wail that the dreaded Carlisle curse was coming true. Frankly, a deserted château in France sounded rather appealing.'' Monty leaned back and shook her head, letting her mane of chestnut hair catch the sunlight and whatever breeze that blew. "By the time I got around to having second thoughts, I was halfway here."

"I didn't know you were in so much trouble."

Eve's dry tone made Monty laugh. "Tactful, Eve, but unnecessary. The debate raged for nearly a week. You couldn't have helped but overhear the whole range of arguments. I don't know why you didn't just resign on the spot."

"Well . . . I need this job."

Monty sobered, acknowledging the abrupt entrance of the candid truth. She wondered when, exactly, Edwin had begun to hire secretaries who were expected to serve double duty as her friend. "You've worked with me for what . . . four, five months, now? Do I pay you well?"

Eve looked at her house slippers. "It's been almost five months and I make a very good wage. But I enjoy working for you, Miss Carlisle. Really, I do."

Monty leveled a caustic gaze at her companion. "One more slip of the tongue like that and you're going to enjoy working for someone else. Remember, my name is Eve and your name is . . . ?''

Eve squinched her lips into a frown and then relaxed them with a resigned sigh. ''Is it really *Montgomery?*''

''My great-great-grandmother's maiden name. We Carlisles are required by law to pass the family names from generation to generation. Which is the reason I've decided to remain celibate.''

Eve's eyes widened. ''You'll have to name your child Montgomery, too?''

''No, by constitutional amendment my child would be named Napoléon, but my grandchildren would be Montgomerys—every single one of them. Montgomery VI, VII or XXII, whatever the appropriate numeral might be. Scary thought, isn't it?''

Eve's eyebrows drew together in a frown. ''That could get very confusing.''

Monty turned back to the scenic view, wishing her secretary had a sense of humor and that she could relax enough to share a laugh with her now and again.

''I do wish you'd move away from that ledge,'' Eve said. ''If anything were to happen to you while we were here, I'd never forgive myself.''

''What could happen?'' Monty leaned out and looked straight down. The drop to the rock terrace that lay between the château and the gardens below was deadly. A fall from this height was nothing to joke about, but there was no point in admitting that to a 'fraidy cat like Eve. ''I'd land smack dab in the middle of a big bramble bush and wind up with a few scratches and a big bruise on my dignity. You worry too much.''

''But the Carlisle curse . . . ?''

''Is nonsense. Like all the other stories Aunt Josephine tells. Besides, the very reason they sent me here was so I'd live to see my twenty-seventh birthday. Or does the curse say I'm supposed to meet a tragic end *on* my twenty-seventh birthday? I forget.'' She clasped her hands and breathed in the delicious smell of the morning. ''Come out here, Eve, and look at the gardens. I'll bet they were really beautiful once.'' She pointed to a thick row of unkempt hedge. ''Look, I think that's a maze, even though it seems a little out of place here. Come on, take a look for yourself.''

Eve made no move to come closer. ''You could get lost in a maze.''

''I could get lost trying to find a bathroom in this mausoleum.''

''There's one off my room,'' Eve said. ''At least the plumbing seems to work all right. Thank heavens one of your ancestors saw fit to modernize this section of the château.''

''My grandparents lived here for a number of years. I believe my parents spent part of their honeymoon here, as well. But when they died, the château was all but forgotten.''

''Do you remember your parents at all?''

Monty shook her head. ''I was only three when my parents were killed and my mother's sister, my Aunt

Josephine, and her husband, Edwin Talbot, came to live in the Carlisle estate in California to take care of me. Edwin was named as my guardian, and he's managed the Carlisle holdings all these years. I'm a little surprised he didn't sell this château years ago.''

"There can't be much of a market for a place like this. It's very run-down.''

Monty nodded and thought it was a wonder the place hadn't collapsed long ago. "I didn't even know this was part of the Carlisle holdings until a few weeks ago.'' She rested her forearms on the banister and made another visual tour of the gardens. "I think I'll talk to Edwin about having some restoration work done and opening the castle to the public... if it isn't too late to make amends for past neglect, that is.''

"I doubt Edwin will allow you to spend a fortune just to ease your conscience.''

Monty caught a glimpse of movement, and suddenly Sebastian was standing in the garden below. Her heartbeat made an unfamiliar skip before settling into a quick, excited rhythm as she watched him stoop and begin pulling weeds from a section of the garden.

He was wearing white this morning—a shirt, buttoned only partially up the front, with the sleeves cuffed and rolled halfway up his forearms. Quite a contrast to the golden brown of his skin. The black jeans he wore stretched taut across his thighs and tucked neatly about his hips. His dark hair was pulled back and clipped carelessly into a short ponytail at his nape. He looked more like a buccaneer than a gardener; more like a Renaissance man than a figment of her imagination. She wondered if he was close enough to hear her should she call to him; wondered if he might know what she was thinking.

Sebastian. She focused all her attention on gaining his. *Sebastian. Remember last night? Look up, Sebastian. Look at me.*

But he didn't look up, didn't act as if he knew she was anywhere near, much less as if he could read her thoughts. So much for telepathy. Bending down, she picked up a pebble from the balcony and tossed it over the rail, missing him by a quarter of a mile. She tried again, but managed merely to ruffle the composure of a leafy plant several feet away. She glanced behind her for something else to throw. "Give me your house slipper, Eve."

"What?"

"Your slipper. Give it to me."

"But, my feet will get cold."

"It will be a noble sacrifice."

The next moment, Monty had the flimsy scuff in her hand and had it aimed at Sebastian's broad back. Launched, it flipped once, then fluttered harmlessly to land in the upper limbs of a scraggly fir tree. "Damn. Give me the other one."

Eve sighed as she handed over the remaining slipper. "Wouldn't it be easier to yell at him?"

"A Carlisle may shout, Eve, but we never yell." Monty stripped a wide gold ring from her finger and tied the flexible scuff around it, making a fair-size missile. She leaned over the rail, sighted her target and threw, nailing Sebastian neatly between the shoulder blades.

He casually turned and looked up. His dark eyes met hers and for a few brief, reckless moments, she felt her heart being pulled inexorably and inevitably into his possession. The very thought frightened her, even as she laughed at herself for having such a vivid imagination.

"Bonjour, Sebastian," she called, raising her voice in order to reach him. "I dropped my shoe."

"Bonjour, mademoiselle." His tone was light, friendly, his smile a pleasant degree of warm. There wasn't a trace of intimacy, not a hint that he had been in this same garden staring up at her on this very balcony only hours before. He reached back and picked up the balled-up house slipper, tossing it once and catching it in his hand. "I believe I've located your slipper."

"Good work." She cupped her hands to form a pseudo catcher's mitt. "Throw it back."

The curve of his lips widened as he gave the "shoe ball" another playful toss and caught it. "I'll keep it safe, *mademoiselle,* until you can retrieve it."

"Merci." She pointed to the fir. "The other one is over there."

He looked, then nodded as if a blush pink scuff was just another blossom in his garden. "I will rescue it, as well," he said. *"C'est un matin delicieux, oui?"*

Lovely, delicious morning. Yes. Monty opened her mouth to answer, but the response that hovered, in perfect French, on the tip of her tongue was interrupted by Eve. "Will you show us the gardens after breakfast?" she asked in English.

He dipped his head in that subservient bow that was anything but submissive. "At your pleasure, Mademoiselle Carlisle."

He turned back to his work, and Monty tapped her fingertip against the cold stone banister. "Sebastian?" she called, waiting until he looked over his shoulder and directly up at her. "Will you take us through the maze, too?"

"It isn't safe."

She flashed a daring smile. "Don't worry, I'll bring my guardian angel along."

She turned away from the balcony, and Seb sank back onto his heels. He examined the knotted house slipper, unwrapping it from around the solid object inside. A ring tumbled into his palm, a wide, heavy band bearing a crest worn smooth with age.

He placed the ring on his fingertip and held it up, letting the sunlight find its reflection in the gold. The ring looked too big for her hand and too expensive to belong to a simple secretary. Yet she'd tossed it about as if it were of no more significance than an apple core, thrown it for no better reason than to gain his attention.

As if he hadn't already been aware of her presence on the balcony above, already been aware of her intense concentration on him. He slipped the ring into his shirt pocket, wiped the back of his hand across his forehead and then tugged the rolled cuff of his white shirt down and over the angry scrape that crisscrossed his forearm. She was getting under his skin, that one, creating a disturbance in his universe, tempting him to forget who he was and why he was here.

There were moments enough, as it was, when he doubted the wisdom of this venture, wondered what he was trying to prove—and to whom. He'd all but killed himself in his attempt to reach the tower room the previous night. And he had nothing but sore muscles and a scraped arm to show for his effort.

Montgomery Carlisle.

The name brought a familiar twist of resentment and anger, as it always did. And as he always did, he forced the feelings down, into the shape of determination. He was going to find what was rightfully his . . . if it existed. And if it did exist, no Carlisle was going to cheat him out of it.

She was a Carlisle. The last descendant of the man who had stolen the de Vergille honor. Did she honestly think she had fooled him? It was so obvious that she, and not the brown-haired mouse, was the heiress. His initial impression had been the right one—the mouse was too backward, too quiet, too afraid to be the flamboyant Montgomery Carlisle. While the red-haired Eve O'Halloran was too confident, too demanding, too compelling to be anyone else. She was an American princess. He was a gardener.

Seb yanked a weed from the damp earth, tossed it aside and reached the same conclusion as he had the night before. Montgomery Carlisle was dangerous. With a snap of her fingers she could ruin his plans, stop his nightly excursions through the silent, secret tunnels that ran throughout the château. For all he knew, she could be part of the insidious theft of the château's long-held treasures—the tapestries, the furnishings, the paintings—that were disappearing with increasing frequency. And it was up to him to keep her occupied until he did know.

Seb could think of only one way to keep his eye on her while diverting her attention from his true purpose. He would persuade her to fall desperately in love with him. As Charlotte had suggested, he had much to gain from such a liaison, and the element of a small but sweet revenge against a Carlisle was not without appeal. The seduction, itself, was hardly an onerous prospect. Certainly the chemistry was already at work between them. With hardly any effort, he could recall the way she had trembled in his arms, the feel of her body against his as he'd held her there in the hallway, the sweet, sweet scent of her hair, its silken texture against his chin. He could visualize her standing on the dark balcony, her lovely body yearning for a man's caress. Yes, romancing her was the obvious solution...no matter what happened to his foolish heart when she looked into his eyes.

MONTY APPROACHED THE maze as she did everything else—as a personal challenge. "All right, Seb. Would you care to make a small wager on how long it will take me to find my way through?"

"Ten francs says you'll be in and out in ten minutes."

"Five francs says I can do it in five."

"If we keep going this way, there'll be no bet at all and you won't have to step inside the maze, to boot."

Monty put her hands on her hips and looked up at him. "You don't talk like a French gardener."

"Dans le jardin, tu es une fleur entre les épines."

She laughed. "Translate, *s'il vous plaît.*"

"You have dirt on your nose."

She scrubbed her hand across the tip of her nose, although she knew exactly what he had said. *In the garden, you are a flower among thorns.* "There," she said. "Is it gone?"

He rubbed his fingertip along the bridge of her nose and then extended the slow stroke into a caress of her cheek, leaving a trail of tantalizing sensation on her skin. "Gone. Vanished, just like Mademoiselle Carlisle."

"You frightened her intentionally, Sebastian, telling her the maze was haunted before she'd taken two bites of her croissant."

"Ah, I should have told her after she'd eaten the roll."

"You should save the ghost stories for me." Monty looked at the overgrown hedge before her. "Now, are you going to show me the way through the maze, or do I have to manage on my own?"

He shook his head. "It isn't safe."

"Give it up, Sebastian. I'm not afraid of anything."

"Perhaps I am afraid, *mademoiselle*. Afraid of you."

She met his dark eyes and allowed his flirtation to fizz inside her like the effervescence of good champagne. "Come now. I don't look anything like the big, bad wolf."

His smile was as smooth as satin. "And therein lies the problem."

"Don't worry. You're perfectly safe with me." She swept her hand in a free-flowing gesture toward the hedge. "After you."

"Never say I didn't give you fair warning." He reached down and closed his hand around hers before pushing back a leggy branch and stepping inside the maze.

Warm exhilaration rippled from her fingertips all the way to her toes as he guided her into the cloistered halls of shrubbery. There was just room for single file between the hedgerows, but Seb didn't offer to release her hand. She used her free arm to push back the more aggressive branches. "It certainly is confining in here, isn't it?"

"In several places the path is completely overgrown."

"I'm surprised there's a path left at all. This maze looks like it's been as badly neglected as the rest of the château."

"You'll notice I have done some trimming in here."

"I noticed there isn't much in the way of topiary."

"Sculpting hedges and trees into recognizable shapes takes more years than I have to invest in the château gardens." He ducked under a brushy arbor. "I'm doing what I can to restore the gardens to a portion of their nineteenth-century charm, and then I dedicate a couple of hours of my day to doing minor repairs inside the château. I don't know how Louis has managed to keep the place from falling apart these past several years. It's just a pity that Mademoiselle Carlisle isn't interested in financing a complete restoration."

Monty hoped he hadn't felt the slight jerk of her hand in his. "I wouldn't say she's not interested."

He laughed. "Wouldn't you? Look around. Her *interest* is evident. This is just one more possession among many others."

"Has it occurred to you that she may have been unaware of the need before now?"

"Frankly, no. Castles don't come cheap and saying that the château needs maintenance is redundant."

"That doesn't mean she's indifferent. She just wasn't . . . um . . . fully apprised of the château's condition."

He squeezed her hand and turned a corner in the maze. "Mademoiselle Carlisle is fortunate to have such a loyal employee."

"Employees are about all she does have, even if they're in scarce supply around here."

"Spare me the 'poor little rich girl' theme. Montgomery Carlisle can have anything she wants."

The words stung, despite their familiarity. "Cliché or not, there are some things that can't be bought."

"Perhaps." He kicked aside a dead branch in their path. "And some things are not for sale, either. She has had any number of offers to purchase the château. All were refused outright."

"No." Monty couldn't imagine that having happened. "Why, I would have…I mean, anyone in their right mind would jump at an offer to get rid of this place."

He turned another corner, doubled back and then brought her into a clearing in which sat a deteriorating and sad-looking gazebo. Wildflowers and weeds grew through the random flooring in small, bold patches of color. Seb released her hand before walking up the worn stone steps and bracing his hand on one of the two remaining support posts. "This is the pavilion," he said. "There are stories told that on dark, moonless nights the ghost of the last chatelaine can be seen wandering here."

"Is she lost? Did she die trying to find her way out of the maze?"

"The maze wasn't built until after her death. She was murdered here in the pavilion."

"Being murdered would certainly make me want to haunt a place." Monty reached down and laid her palm flat against one of the cold, smooth stones. "Who killed her?"

"Some say it was her lover, that he begged her to run away with him. Perhaps she was tempted to go. That part of the story no one knows. But she was aware that while society could forgive her for taking a lover, desertion of her family would never be pardoned. She couldn't bring scandal into the lives of her husband and children, so she refused to go with him. And he killed her."

Monty straightened and rubbed her hands together, trying to defeat the chill that had seeped into her skin. "A hot-blooded Frenchman, no doubt."

"*Au contraire,* a cold-blooded American. Josiah Carlisle."

Surprised, Monty turned. "I find that hard to believe."

"Why? Did you know him?"

"Of course not. But I've heard about him for as long as . . . well, since I started working for Miss Carlisle." She shrugged, telling herself she had no personal investment in this story. "He just doesn't sound like the kind of man who would have murdered someone. Especially not a woman."

"And what kind of man commits murder? Or would you find it easier to believe if the victim had been a man?"

She had no answer for the first question, and the second didn't deserve one. She told him so with a delicate arching of her eyebrows. "You said *some* people think the murderer was her lover. Does that mean there's disagreement about how the chatelaine came to her untimely end?"

Sebastian sat on the step and rested his arms on upraised knees. He was a fascinating specimen of a man and Monty could hardly tear her eyes away from him. "Her husband was a man of passion and there were many who believed he was responsible for her murder, that he discovered her with her lover and killed her in the heat of anger. In either case, Edouard, her husband, bore the guilt, even though there was never any proof that he committed the crime."

"No smoking guns were left at the scene, I take it." Monty brushed dirt from the step and sat next to Seb, not so close as to touch him but near enough to create a small rise in her body temperature. "There probably wasn't much in the way of scientific investigation at the time, either."

"But there were plenty of opinions. Especially after Edouard fled the country. None of the stories gives his reasons—whether he ran away to escape punishment, whether he went in search of revenge upon the lover, who had so conveniently returned to America, or if he was trying to elude the thought of life without his beloved Lily. Whatever his reasoning, he paid a dear price, for when he returned to the château several years later he found his home had been sold to his enemy, Josiah Carlisle.''

"His wife's lover.''

Sebastian nodded. "Edouard's son believed his father was guilty of murdering his mother and that he would never return to France—if he were even still alive. The family fortunes had taken a downward spiral with the scandal, and the son, Hugh, was glad to be rid of the place in which his mother had died so violently. He, of course, didn't know there had been another man, much less his identity. For Edouard, losing the château was a mortal blow. Carlisle had stolen everything...wife, home, honor. There was nothing left for him, and he jumped to his death from the south tower only days later.''

Monty studied the toes of her shoes. "Does he haunt the château?''

Seb turned his dark gaze to her face. "Wouldn't you?''

"Absolutely. Especially if there were a Carlisle in residence.''

"Does the thought frighten you?''

It did, oddly enough. Somehow, the ghost was a personal enemy now, with reason enough to want revenge on any heir of Josiah Carlisle. "Is he dangerous?''

Seb gave a little shrug. "Perhaps, after all these years, he's simply lonely.''

"If he's haunting the château and she's haunting the garden, I don't see why he'd be lonely."

"Her blood is on his hands. When he found her here and realized she was dead, he filled his hands with her blood and held it up to the heavens, begging for her life to be restored. But when he opened his fists, the blood had been changed into rubies, as cold and lifeless as her body. He flung them out into the garden and ran away. The rubies blossomed overnight into this maze . . . a maze Edouard's ghost cannot enter and Lily's ghost can never leave." A rueful smile touched Seb's lips. "At least, that's the way the legend is told."

The breeze echoed a faraway sigh, and Monty rubbed a shiver from her arms. "Wouldn't Aunt Josephine have a field day with that one."

"Who?"

Monty gave a little start. "Oh, uh, Aunt Josephine. Miss Carlisle's aunt. Everybody calls her that . . . Aunt, I mean. Aunt Josephine." He frowned and Monty stood abruptly, dusting the seat of her pants with the palms of her hands. "So, what did you say their names were? The ghosts. Edouard and . . . ?"

"Lily de Vergille. My great-great-grandparents."

"De Vergille? Then this . . . the château . . . it belongs to your family? To you?"

Seb looked up at her for a long moment before he pushed to his feet and towered over her by at least a foot. "This is the Château Carlisle, *mademoiselle*. I have no claim to put forth, other than that I hope to see the château restored and cared for.''

Which was an out-and-out lie, Monty thought. He had a claim. A claim of heritage and birth that no legal document could annul. Whether or not the story of Lily's murder was true as he'd told it, Sebastian had cause to hate anyone by the name of Carlisle. She was the rightful heir to his anger, and he wouldn't be looking at her the way he was at this moment if he knew her true identity.

And she wanted him to keep looking at her in that special way. She wanted that very badly. "You must hate Montgomery Carlisle," she said helplessly. "She doesn't care a fig for what should have been yours."

His smile was gently amused. "I thought you said she was simply unaware of the need."

"That's true. Really." Monty knew she sounded overly sincere, overly eager to have him believe her, but it was so very important that he did. "She doesn't pay much attention to possessions, doesn't consider them important, and sometimes . . . a lot of times, I suppose . . . that might make her appear indifferent."

He looked deeply into her eyes, and she thought her legs were going to buckle under the intense excitement that whipped through her. Then slowly he lifted his hand and drew the backs of his fingers across her cheek, heightening the intensity to a confusing need. "You are a devoted assistant, *mademoiselle*, but you shouldn't feel you have to defend your employer. I, too, am paid with Carlisle money."

She caught his hand and held it against her skin for a moment, thrilling with the contact. "Why are you here, Seb? And please don't try to tell me it has nothing to do with the story of Lily and Edouard and Josiah Carlisle."

"All right, I won't tell you that. I'll say, instead, that since you arrived I'm having a difficult time remembering that my place is in the gardens."

She was disappointed that he reverted to flirtation now, just as she was beginning to think they'd reached a common ground. "I find it hard to believe that you would return to this particular château just to restore the gardens."

"Do you, *mademoiselle?* Would you prefer to believe I'm searching for the lost legacy of my family? Lily's rubies, perhaps. Maybe there is a fortune in jewels hidden inside the château."

"Yes," Monty said without hesitation. "A mission sounds much more exciting."

As quickly as a droll smile edged his lips, he reached into his pocket and pulled out Eve's slippers. "This was my mission." He placed them in her hand and folded her fingers to secure the items. "I have rescued the shoes you misplaced this morning."

"And the ring?"

"Ah, finding that, *mademoiselle,* will have to be your mission."

His soft laughter kindled her smile of response, and she dropped the house slippers to grab his arm. "You have it, Sebastian. Give it to me or I'll have no choice but to search—"

Her fingertips encountered a scaly, heated patch of skin, and she looked down at the abrasion which was just visible below his shirtsleeve. With a frown, she pushed up the rolled cuff and cupped his forearm in both her hands. "What happened to you?"

He shrugged and pulled away, rolling down his sleeve as he did so. "The hazards of working with overgrown hedgerows."

"That looks like a bad scrape, not just a scratch."

Her regard made him edgy for a second, and then he smiled. "My mission was fraught with danger, *mademoiselle*. One of your shoes was in a tree, but I gladly suffered injury for you."

That injury hadn't happened in the past hour, she thought. But Seb obviously didn't trust her enough to confide in her—at least, not yet. "I would do the same for you," she said lightly. "If you asked."

He turned away, and while he studied the remains of the pavilion, she studied him, measuring the width of his shoulders with her eyes, gauging his thoughts by the tension emanating from him, wondering how his lips would feel pressed against hers. That odd electric feeling stole through her, the same mystifying sense of destiny she'd experienced the previous night on the balcony. A feeling that whoever Sebastian was and whatever he was doing in this place, she was bound to him in a way she couldn't as yet understand.

The atmosphere at the center of the maze grew thick as her breathing grew shallow and slow. When finally he turned to her, she could almost believe he was unaware of her tension. His expression was relaxed and easy, his gaze softly toying with her heartbeat. And then he spoke to her in a husky whisper. *"Je t'embrasse."*

His words bathed her in tiny thrills. He was going to kiss her. She couldn't breathe, much less move. Had he read her thoughts? Did he see the desire in her eyes?

Or was he, like she, caught in the undertow of a chemistry that had taken them both by surprise? A chemistry too powerful to fight. He had just said he was going to kiss her, and all she could think to whisper in response was a throaty *"Vive la France!"*

His smile was worth waiting for, and she stood her ground, unable to be the aggressor, requesting him to make the move. He stepped closer, and placing his hands on her shoulders, he drew her toward him. Fascinated by the shape of his lips, Monty couldn't have looked away if Lily's ghost had tapped her on the shoulder. She was in another plane, another world, as he lowered his head slowly...oh, so slowly...and claimed her first with the moist, heady warmth of his breath and then with the oh-so-perfect touch of his lips.

A warm, liquid languor spilled through her body, fueled by his eager but tender possession. Monty realized with pleasurable surprise that kissing Sebastian was even more exciting than the anticipation of it.

Why, her body fairly ached with excitement, and her heart soared in a rhythmic flight as her senses spun with the exquisite feel of his kiss. She clung to him, allowing her arms to slip around him, to hold him in an embrace she did not want to end.

And when, inevitably, it did, she pulled him back for a second taste of heaven.

THE TOWER HAD an unencumbered view of the pavilion, and a minor adjustment of the binoculars brought two figures into focus. Sebastian de Vergille and Montgomery Carlisle. Star-crossed lovers stealing a kiss in the garden. How sweet.

So, Sebastian was making his move. And Monty, the silly girl, was dying for a little excitement.

Dying for excitement.

Now, that was funny.

Chapter Four

"What are you doing?" Eve's question resounded down the hall like gossip passing from one angel to the next.

Monty jerked upright and narrowly missed hitting her head on the edge of the marble pedestal. "I was just, uh, looking around. You know, checking out the scene of the crime."

"Crime?" Eve's voice held a quiver, and Monty was quick to reassure her.

"Merely a figure of speech," she said. "I wanted to see the hall in daylight and figure out exactly how I managed to knock off an angel."

"The statue is gone."

"Right down to the halo. I've just been standing here wondering if Charlotte propped the thing in a closet somewhere. What is the proper procedure for disposing of a fallen angel?"

"I don't see how she could have lifted it by herself."

"Pecs of steel," Monty said with a nod. "Didn't you notice the muscle on that woman?"

Eve frowned, then looked at the floor. "At least she swept up all the fragments and got rid of the mess. It's obvious that she's better with a broom than with a frying pan."

Memory collected on the back of Monty's tongue like the greasy taste of breakfast, and she swallowed. "Tell her that from now on we'll have croissants from the local baker and coffee, for our morning meal. If we'd wanted ham hocks and fried eggs, we'd have gone to Kansas, not France."

"I'll tell her, but I'm not sure it will do any good." Eve touched the pedestal with one hesitant finger. "This looks so empty. Do you think the statue can be replaced? You should ask Edwin about it."

"I'll add that to my list of questions." Monty wanted to continue her search for hidden doors in the second-floor hall, and she wished Eve would go on about her business. "I suppose there's no way to avoid telling Edwin that I was the one who clumsily bumped against the statue and made it fall."

"It wasn't your fault that Charlotte raced off with the lantern, leaving us alone in the dark." Eve's sigh was soft and self-sacrificing. "You ought to fire her for causing so much difficulty, Miss Carlisle. And pain. I'll bet you have a horrible bruise."

"Bruise?"

"From bumping up against this. I mean, these statues must weigh a hundred pounds. Maybe more.

And if you hit the pedestal hard enough to knock the statue off balance..."

A bruise. Monty didn't know why she hadn't thought of it sooner. Perhaps Eve had a trace of bloodhound in her, after all. Someone around here had a bruised shoulder. Unless, of course... But, no, she didn't believe the statue had been pushed from its base. The whole thing had been an accident.

"You know, it's odd, the statue falling the way it did." Eve tucked a strand of hair behind her ear, a nervous habit Monty had noticed many times before. "I mean, if you bumped against the pedestal from this side, wouldn't the statue have fallen in the other direction instead of toward the windows? Toward where you were standing?"

With Eve's innocent words, Monty wrestled a chill. "Will you stop imagining things? I bumped the pedestal. The angel wobbled around and fell over. It was an accident."

"You don't believe any of the talk about..." Eve bit her lower lip. "Ghosts?"

Fear vanished like a shooting star, as Monty wavered between impatience and laughter. "Honestly, Eve. You're getting almost as paranoid as Aunt Jo. Don't you have a letter to write or a book to read or something you need to do?" Monty waved in the direction of the stairs. "Go on. I want to do a little exploring on my own."

The expected protest poured readily from Eve's lips. "You shouldn't be wandering around this place by yourself. It simply isn't safe. I'll stay with you."

"That isn't necessary."

"It's no trouble. I really don't like being alone here, anyway."

Monty tapped out her annoyance with her fingers on top of the pedestal, knowing Eve would stick to her like glue for the rest of the afternoon. Of course, she could order the poor woman to leave her alone, but she knew in her heart that any such order would be ignored. Clearly, Eve felt responsible and had decided it was her duty to keep a watchful eye on her employer... no matter what that employer had to say about it.

With a shrug, Monty turned toward the stairway and the great hall below. "Come on, then. I want to take another look at the maze. There's a pavilion in the center, and Sebastian told me this wonderful... well, actually, it's an *awful* story about a murder there years and years ago. The chatelaine was killed and her blood spilled all over everything, and now her ghost wanders the maze and can't get out. I'll tell you the story as we go." She trotted down the stairs and smiled at the sound of Eve's footsteps dragging reluctantly along behind her.

"CONFESS, UNCLE EDWIN. You're trying to make my life miserable."

His chuckle crossed the overseas line as easily as it would have crossed the room to reach her. "Hello, Monty, dear. How nice to hear from you. Are you enjoying your vacation at the château?"

"I'm having a smashing time," she said. "Wish you were here."

"To share your misery? That's sweet, Monty, but I have my hands full of misery right here at home, trying to settle your account with Stanton Grainger."

"Give him the ruby and your troubles are over."

Edwin was a man of eloquent sighs, and this one lost nothing in the translation from southern California to the lush Loire Valley. "Life is always so simple for you, Monty."

"Life here at the château is beautifully simple. We're not bothered with complicated things such as electricity or maid service or meals that require more than a hand-cranked can opener and a spoon."

"What's wrong with the electricity?"

"The wires are crossed. Or the generator's haunted. How should I know? It was all I could do to find my way to my bedroom in the dark last night."

"What?" His irritation snapped through the phone line.

"I said, it was all I could—"

"I heard what you said. Where's the caretaker and the rest of those people I told him to hire?"

"They're not here."

"Louis isn't there?"

"No."

"Well, where the hell is he?"

"Away on business." Monty twisted the phone cord around her little finger, finding perverse satisfaction in knowing Edwin was now upset.

"The château *is* his business. What is he thinking, being away when he knows you were arriving?"

"Apparently, he's thinking he has business elsewhere."

"And just what do you find so amusing? I can't believe there isn't any electricity. Frankly, I'm surprised you didn't call and scream at me last night."

"It took me this long to find the phone, and I'm not screaming...yet."

A pause. "All right, Monty. You fooled me for a moment, but I'm on to you now. Where are you, really? Paris? Côte d'Azur?"

She laughed. "I'm at the château. What's the matter? Are you finding it difficult to imagine me without a few of life's little luxuries?"

"Not difficult, Monty, impossible. But for the sake of argument, I'll pretend that you have actually done what you were supposed to do...for once in your life. You're at the château. The caretaker is away on business. Who is there to take care of you?"

"I can take care of myself."

His pause was deliberately skeptical. "Yes, of course you can, Monty. But satisfy my curiosity, please. Who, besides Eve, is there at the château with you?"

"There's a gardener, Sebastian, and then there's Charlotte. I haven't figured out what her job is, but I've eliminated several possibilities so far."

"Charlotte is Louis's American wife," he explained tersely. "She helps take care of the château. I just can't understand why he isn't there. I spoke to him only a day or so ago, and he didn't mention anything about being away from the château when you arrived."

"What did you expect him to say? 'Oh, I don't think I can be here then'?"

"That would have been preferable to not making an appearance at all. His absence is inexcusable. I'll dismiss him. And as soon as we conclude this call, I'll see what I can do about the electricity."

"You're quite the wizard, Edwin."

"Why? Because I know who to call in an emergency?"

"I can't imagine that the American ambassador will be much help in getting the electricity back on, but call whoever you want. The gardener says the local power station has trouble every time there's a storm—as there was last night—and the generator here is old and unreliable."

"And the caretaker isn't there to fix it. I'm sorry, Monty. I thought the château would provide a nice hideaway for you."

As if she needed a place to hide. She hoped Stanton Grainger ended up with Joan's ruby, one way or another. "Don't worry about the electricity, Edwin. At the moment, I'm more concerned with the reason the château has been allowed to deteriorate as it has."

"Deteriorate? Why, that's nonsense, Monty. I've authorized thousands of dollars for improvements, not to mention the fortune spent every year on staff and general maintenance."

"The money hasn't gone into the château, Edwin. At least, not much of it. I'm embarrassed that the castle has been so sadly neglected, and I want you to do something about it."

"I will, Monty. I'm going to fire Louis and get an honest, trustworthy caretaker."

She looked out the window at the grounds that swept like a rolling wave into the valley and the town below. "I want the château restored, Edwin. Completely restored. And I want a trust established to ensure that future needs are met. Do whatever is necessary, but see that it's done."

"All right." His tone was cautious, as if he thought she would give him the punch line at any moment. "Château restored. Anything else?"

"Get a pencil and paper. The list starts with a service staff and ends with a couple of bicycles. And Edwin, keep in mind that I never would have seen the château if you and Aunt Jo hadn't insisted."

"This is for your own good, Monty."

"So you've said before. I'm here. I'll stay until my birthday, if only to prove to Aunt Josephine that her moronic Carlisle curse is a morbid fantasy and that she's a certified space cadet. But in the meantime, a few changes will have to be made here at Château Carlisle. And that, Edwin, is where you come in.''

"It always is.''

Monty smiled and began to list the 'luxuries' she couldn't live without.

THE MEMORY OF Sebastian's kiss followed Monty into a night of seductive dreams. He was there, no matter where the dream began or what other presence passed through the shadowy world of her sleep. He held her, gathering her close in his arms, pressing his lips against her hair, her eyes, her cheek, her mouth. His voice was in her mind, his whisper a gentle sensation in her ear.

Monty.

Turning in her sleep, she grappled with consciousness, wanting to stay lost in the dreams, snuggled into the safety and pleasure of a remembered embrace.

Monty.

But wait, he didn't know her by that name. *"I'm Eve,"* she whispered into the dream. *"I'm an ordinary secretary. I work for a living. I'm paid with Carlisle money, just like you. We're ordinary. Plain, ordinary people. That's why we're so good at kissing."*

As if to prove the statement, his lips brushed her temple in a warm caress, then moved lower to initiate a fleeting but debilitating kiss on her lips. Within the gossamer web of sleep, Monty responded, placing her arms around his neck to pull him further into the dream. But her arms closed on empty air and a chill invaded her whole body, bringing her abruptly awake.

"Well, that was rude," she murmured huskily and reached for the elusive comforter that had slipped halfway off the bed.

"Pardonnez moi." His voice was like the darkness around her, soft, thick and indistinct.

Monty grabbed the coverlet and pulled it up to her chin, as she tried to see past the blackness and hear over the sudden heavy pounding of her heart. "Wh-who's there?" she called faintly, like some lily-livered heroine in a gothic novel. "W-what do you want?"

Sebastian appeared at the foot of the bed, a wry smile gracing the corners of his mouth. "I didn't mean to frighten you, but when I saw you asleep my wits deserted me, and I couldn't think of how I might explain my presence here in your bedchamber."

She wiggled into a sitting position while she gathered her own wits about her. Having the man of her dreams appear at the foot of her bed in the dark of night had never seemed a viable possibility before. She didn't quite know what she expected to happen next. "Sebastian?"

"Oui."

She released her breath in a rush. "I was just making sure you were the gardener and not the ghost."

His laughter crept beneath the covers to caress her. "I assure you, *mademoiselle,* I am very real."

She thought she might have been safer with the ghost. "How did you get in here, Seb?"

"I came to tell you."

"You're here to tell me that you can wander in and out of my bedroom whenever you choose?"

"I came through the passageway and entered your room there." He pointed into the darkness, and Monty strained to see an entrance which eluded her. "I am here to ask for your assistance."

She dropped one fold of the coverlet and then grabbed it back in her fist. "My assistance with what?"

"To explore the château. To discover, if we can, the hidden treasure."

Maybe she was still asleep. This was beginning to sound a little like the Joan-of-Arc-and-the-ruby story. Monty rubbed her eyes, then reached for the candlestick and the small box of matches on the bedside table. She lit one of the candles and was reassured by the flicker of light that spread in a soft puddle around the bed.

The illumination of Seb, standing tall and dark and mysterious at the foot of the bed, wasn't so reassuring. Not that she thought he would harm her. No, quite the contrary. At this precise moment, she was afraid he might disappear again without having laid a hand on her.

"Wait a minute." She cleared her throat of a disturbing ache, and tried to sound like a woman who was accustomed to having midnight discussions with a real, live man instead of a bedpost. "I thought you said I'd been reading too many fairy tales, that there were no secret passageways."

He shrugged. "I found one."

"Just stumbled across it, did you?"

He wrapped one hand around the bedpost, and his gaze found her in the dusky light. "Do you wish to go with me?"

Follow this man through a dark tunnel in the middle of the night? "Sure," she said. "Why not? Hand me those clothes." She indicated an assortment of clothing strewn across a Louis Quatorze chair. "And there should be a pair of shoes around here somewhere." Extending the candlelight over the edge of the bed, she leaned out and pointed at the floor. "There's one. Oh, and there's the other one, beside the armoire. See it?"

He bent to pick up the closer shoe, and Monty moved the candle to gain a better view. The light defined the muscular line of his hips and legs, the taut pull of black cloth over thighs that bunched and then stretched with supple power. He moved like a leopard, every action choreographed in grace, every nuance of motion a study of efficiency and form.

After getting the other shoe, he turned toward her, and Monty told herself to pick her chin up off the floor before she embarrassed both of them. The candlelight flickered, betraying her, and she set the candlestick back on the table with a hurried, self-conscious movement.

With a flourish, he set the shoes on the rug beside the bed. "I have rescued your footwear twice today, *mademoiselle*. Perhaps, I should have a reward."

Her heart ached with disappointment. If Seb was already asking compensation for services rendered . . .

He picked up the blouse and dark jeans she had tossed onto the chair before going to bed and handed them to her. She reached for the clothes, but he held on when she went to take them from his grasp, creating a little game of tug-of-war. "I noticed you smuggling croissants from the kitchen after the evening meal. As a reward for my assistance with your footwear, you will share the contraband with me." His shoulders lifted in a shrug of understated charm. "Charlotte is not so good with *la cuisine.*"

Monty laughed, delighted that his idea of a reward was so simple. Of course she was an idiot, overly sensitive and too quick to jump to conclusions. She was going to have to start thinking like a hired hand and not like a woman who never asked the balance in her checking account. "I already ate the rolls," she said apologetically. "But tomorrow I'll smuggle out a couple for you."

"That would be kind." His gaze delved deeply into hers, and a blush of no small proportions rose up her neck and into her cheeks. For all she knew, he could have commanded her to react so. Certainly, her body seemed eager to obey any directive he might want to give.

She tightened her grip on the clothing, wondering if she could possibly be feeling the warmth of his touch across several inches of fabric. "It would be kind, Sebastian, if you would turn your back so I can get dressed."

"Kind to you, perhaps, but not kind to me."

He didn't alter his position or his gaze and her blush turned inward, racing through her veins like hot, slick syrup. She grabbed the jeans, stuffed them under the covers and twisted her body until she managed to insert both feet into and through the appropriate leg openings. From there, it was a simple matter of bucking and wiggling until she maneuvered the jeans over her hips and into position. Once in place, she closed the zipper with smooth satisfaction. The blouse wasn't as difficult, but under the intensity of Sebastian's gaze her fingers fumbled with the buttons. "It isn't easy doing this under the covers, you know."

"You do look uncomfortable."

"If you were a gentleman, you'd turn around."

His smile was deliciously male. "If my attention bothers you, perhaps you should blow out the candle."

And have him watch her under cover of darkness? No, thank you. This was unsettling enough. "I'm dressed now, anyway." She fastened the middle buttons of the blouse and pushed back the coverlet. "Just give me a minute to slip on my shoes, and I'm ready for adventure." She swung her bare feet over the edge of the bed as she pushed her discarded nightgown out of sight beneath her pillow. "So, are we looking for Lily's rubies?"

"Nothing so valuable. We seek a silver chalice."

She arched an eyebrow. "Is that anything like the Holy Grail?"

"A little less than holy, but still the stuff of legend. It is believed that Edouard drank the harvest wine from the chalice before throwing himself off the tower."

Monty slanted her eyes at Seb. "Bad vintage?"

"Broken heart." Seb stepped from behind the bed and offered his hand. "The chalice may be as imaginary as Lily's rubies, but there is mention of it in family records kept before Edouard's death, and I intend to make a diligent effort to search for it."

And wherever he searched, she was going to be right behind him, playing Clark to his Lewis, Robin to his Batman. Placing her hand in his, she first enjoyed the tingle of excitement his touch evoked, then steadied herself as she slid off the mattress and into her shoes. "So what makes you think this silver chalice is hidden in the château?"

He shrugged. "The story has been passed from generation to generation of my family. From the time the first de Vergille harvested grapes in this valley, the chalice was used in the sampling of the wines. It became the symbol of our prosperity, blessed by Bacchus, a talisman of good fortune. When it vanished, so, too, did our destiny."

A powerful talisman, Monty thought. "And your family believes Edouard hid it somewhere in the château before he jumped to his death."

"It's never been more than a theory, but the possibility intrigues me. So I decided while I am working in the home of my ancestors, I will discover, if I can, whether the story is myth, truth or a combination of the two."

She looked into his eyes and her throat tightened with attraction. With all her heart, she hoped he would find what he sought. "And if you don't find the chalice?"

He squeezed her hand and led her away from the bed. "Then I'll pass the legend on to my son...if and when I have one."

A perfect opening for the obvious question. "Are you married, Seb?"

"No. Are you?"

"No. I'm not sure I want to be married. Too many uncertainties."

Stopping halfway across the room, he looked past her to the table beside the bed. "We should take the candles. It's very dark in the passageways." He released her hand and moved quickly to light the remaining candles, then with candlestick in hand, he returned to her side. "What kind of uncertainties?" he asked. "Are you afraid your husband would prove unfaithful?"

Her fears centered more on the possibility that her future husband would prove endlessly faithful to the

Carlisle fortune. "I'm not afraid of anything, remember? That's why I'm about to follow you into a secret tunnel with nothing more than a couple of candles to light the way."

"The radiance of your beauty will guide us."

"Oh, yes, my natural glow. That should take us about three feet before the darkness becomes blinding."

"Never fear, fair maiden. I have a flashlight." He flattened his palm against a section of the wall and it moved slowly, silently, swinging out and into the room, revealing a thin, dark opening. A musty smell tickled Monty's nose. A swirl of dank, cool air curled around her and she sneezed.

A circle of light pierced the gloom as Seb switched on the flashlight and directed the beam into the passageway. "You can change your mind," he said. "I'll understand."

"Don't try to get out of taking me with you, Seb. It's too late for that. You'd be embarking on a lost cause."

His smile curved with an eerie charm in the strange shadows. "You are an unusual woman, Eve O'Halloran."

A thrill ignited Monty's excitement. She kept forgetting that Seb knew her as Eve. He actually believed she was a secretary—an ordinary, everyday person. There was no fortune to blur his vision of her. In his eyes, she was simply a woman. How enchanting to realize that he liked her for herself and for no other reason. Her masquerade, conceived of boredom, seemed suddenly full of new promise. "Lead the way, Sebastian. I have a feeling your Holy Grail is almost within our grasp."

"I hope your feelings are more trustworthy than my own."

He handed her the candlestick and turned sideways to slip through the opening. Taking a deep breath, Monty followed. With candles in hand, she sidled her way into the dark and musty tunnel. The closeness of the walls was inhibiting, practically forcing her to draw slow, deep breaths, but the ceiling seemed to stretch forever over her head. She extended the candlestick and looked down at the dusty planking beneath her feet. "This doesn't look much like the Yellow Brick Road. Should I have worn my ruby slippers?"

"Only if they glow in the dark." He moved forward, away from her, and she felt a sudden chill. "Watch your step as we move through the tunnel."

"Am I going to trip over buried treasures?"

"The flooring is uneven, so you should be careful. There is little danger of finding buried treasure by accident."

"Just the same, I'll keep my eyes peeled for the booty. Is your family missing any other heirlooms?"

His hesitation was sudden and unexpected, but the snap of tension in the air was gone in an instant. "The chalice is the only treasure I seek ... unless I submit to temptation and steal the riches from your lips."

"Now you're beginning to sound like a Frenchman, Seb." She kept her voice light, not wanting him to know that the mere thought of kissing him turned her into a wobbly-kneed ingenue. "Tell me when I'm supposed to swoon from your charm."

"Now is not the time, and this is not the place." He spread the light in a smooth sweep, revealing a narrow passageway that disappeared into a long and vast blackness. "You can swoon later. For now, stay close behind me, but don't set my shirt afire. Any safety features built into the tunnel have long since lost their value."

She held up the candles and squinted curiously at the walls that surrounded her. "How did you discover this?" she asked. "And who built it in the first place?"

"The château has evolved for centuries. It is a blend of architectural styles and influences. Over the years, additions have been made, conveniences added. The passageways were probably built into this wing in the seventeenth century, possibly the early eighteenth. As in England, servants used interior tunnels like this one to reach the bedchambers of the aristocracy who resided there. If you'll look closely at the walls in your room, you'll be able to see how the doors were cut into the wall and are concealed by tapestries or by other wall coverings. They're almost invisible."

"Does every room have access to the tunnel?"

"No, but most of the main rooms do. The passageway connects to the kitchen, the wine cellar, dining rooms, ballroom—any area inside or outside the château, which a servant might have needed to reach quickly to ensure his master's comfort. There is an entrance just below the front steps outside and one that is cut into a high wall near the maze in the garden."

"So that's how you were able to appear and disappear like a wisp of magic the night I arrived. I wondered how you managed to be in two places at once."

"Only a ghost could accomplish such a feat." He moved forward confidently, sure of foot in the murky tunnel.

"Don't play games with me, Sebastian." Monty lifted the candlestick and did her best not to cringe at the sight of a big, woolly spider scurrying away from the light. "I know it was you who rescued me from the falling angel. And now that I know you're familiar with this secret tunnel, I have a fair idea of how you were able to walk through the front door only a few minutes later."

He paused a couple of steps ahead of her, using the flashlight beam to sweep the gloom into innocuous shadows. "Watch your step. The floor is uneven here."

She directed the candle flame to the path in front of her and gingerly took another step. "I'm just hoping the château spiders don't like the taste of American blood."

"I thought you weren't afraid of anything."

"I make an exception for creatures that have more legs than I do."

"They're more frightened of you than you are of them."

"Oh, I don't think so, but if one tries to take a bite out of me, I'll burn the little sucker with hot wax."

Seb laughed softly and shone the flashlight beam on the walls and ceiling around her. "The little 'suckers' are in hiding. You're quite safe."

"Thank you, Sebastian. But before we get too far from the subject, I want to hear you admit that you were in the hall with me when the statue fell."

For a moment she thought he might deny it, but then she saw him lift his shoulder in a careless shrug. "I used the passageway, thinking I could retrieve my flashlight and climbing gear from the hall before it was seen. In my haste, I bumped against the pedestal and the angel fell. It was, as you said, an accident. Luckily, you were not hurt."

"Why would it matter if I saw your climbing gear?" she asked, satisfied that his description of the incident matched her own theory.

"I didn't want Mademoiselle Carlisle to see it." He paused, then continued moving along the narrow passage.

Monty frowned. "Why?"

"The chalice may not even exist except in my family mythology. If in reality it does exist, it can have no meaning for Montgomery Carlisle."

That much was certainly true. "Why not just ask her if you can search for the chalice?"

"I believe she would claim the chalice as a part of the estate. So you can understand why I do not want her to know about the passageway or the chalice." He glanced back at Monty, letting the flashlight beam fall into a pool of light at his feet, leaving his face in shadow, while hers was cast in the glow of the candles. "I hope I have not misplaced my trust by confiding in you . . . Eve."

His use of her name was hesitant, as if he had said it to shift the balance of easy camaraderie and make her aware of him. As if she wasn't completely exhilarated by being so close to him, so intimately sealed off from the rest of the world with him. *Eve.* He'd spoken the name as if it were delicate crystal, and Monty was thrilled to the tips of her toes . . . even if Eve wasn't her name. "You can trust me, Seb," she said, pleased with the idea of keeping his secrets. "Cross my heart and hope to die."

The flashlight brushed across his leg and the light dimmed even further, making him seem mysterious and brooding in the shadows. "I would not want you to die for my secrets, *mademoiselle.* I only wish to regain the heritage that is rightfully mine."

Monty shivered with his somber tone of voice . . . or maybe because of a sudden, shallow gust of chill, dank air. "I wish that, too, Sebastian," she said. "Now, where do we begin the search for this birthright of yours?"

He turned back, swinging the flashlight beam up and over the wall ahead. A second tunnel appeared as an oval abyss, a turn in the darkness and nothing more. "That way lies the door to the north tower, but the stairs are tedious and we will save them for another expedition. First, I will show you the way to the garden."

Sebastian moved on and Monty followed him past the entrance to the second passageway and on through the darkness, noting the sameness of the tunnel as she passed through. Although the closeness had widened to a more comfortable width, the view from point to point was monotonously similar. She felt as if she were walking on a treadmill. "How much farther?" she called, hearing her words echo eerily both ahead and behind her.

Seb answered from several feet in front of her. "It isn't far. The door to the second-floor hallway is just at the foot of these steps."

"Steps?" Monty moved the candlelight and was able to discern the outline of a crude stairway before the flames flared briefly and went out, as if someone had reached out and snuffed them out with a giant hand. "Uh-oh," she murmured. "I hope you brought the matches."

"They are on the table beside your bed." He was suddenly by her side, taking the candlestick from her grasp, as if he could wish the flames back into existence. "I'd better go back and get them."

"Can't we manage with just the flashlight?"

"If we continue, we should have two sources of light . . . in case we are separated or one of the lights is disabled. We can return to your room and explore another night, or you can wait for me here. I can be there and back very quickly."

She gulped. This was either the end of her adventure or the time to back up her claim that she wasn't afraid of anything. "Take the flashlight and go. I'll think of some way to defend myself against the spiders."

He touched her heart with his smile. "I will personally burn any little 'sucker' that dares trouble you in my absence."

She was glad that he appreciated her bravery. "Guide me to the stairs. I'll sit on the top step and wait for you."

Obligingly, he illuminated the top of the stairs and Monty moved to take her place there, as if she were a queen approaching her throne. One glance at the dusty, wooden step, however, and she felt more like the queen's scullery maid. She gave Seb a courageous smile, though, and waved him off. "You won't forget about me, will you?" she queried softly.

He came forward, bringing the light and the warm comfort of his presence. Her fear, so vaguely stated, found reassurance in the way he caught and held her gaze. "I could never forget you, *mademoiselle*. Not in a thousand lifetimes."

His lips claimed hers in a touch as fierce and gentle as a winter fire. The kiss burned the stiffening from the backs of her knees, and she thought she might go up in flames. But like the candles, the flicker of passion was snuffed out all too quickly, and with a faint and final caress, he turned and left her, vanishing by degrees into the dark, the flashlight beam bobbing into nothingness a brief moment later.

As the blackness closed around her, Monty shivered, not knowing whether she was actually cold or merely lonely. Wrapping her arms across her chest, she hugged herself and tried not to think about the eight-legged creatures that might want to make her acquaintance. Suddenly, sitting down didn't seem like such a great idea. Ditto, leaning against the tunnel wall. So, she stood where he had left her and hoped he would hurry.

Thirty seconds into his absence, she began to wonder why she was so certain he would return. What if he had no intention of coming back? What if he left her here, closed in and lost in this narrow tunnel? Would she die before she could find her way out?

"Nonsense," she said aloud and stomped her foot for emphasis. The action felt good and she stomped again, liking the idea that she might at least be terrifying the spiders. Maybe she should sing a chorus of "Frère Jacques." That would really scare their furry socks off.

Before she could frame the first tuneful phrase, she sensed movement behind her and then a swift, firm pressure between her shoulder blades. She fell forward, helplessly propelled into the pitch-black stairwell which sprang up to swallow her.

Chapter Five

Monty was aware of a dull ache in her hip and a vague discomfort in her right palm. She was more acutely aware, however, of Seb's hand smoothing her hair and of his soft foreign voice talking her back to the reality of the uneven stairs in the dark passageway. With a blink and a frown, she struggled up from her half-reclining position and tried to locate a more comfortable way of sitting. Seb moved his arms to support her and the ache in her hip subsided, replaced by the toasty awareness of his strong, muscular and heavenly warm proximity.

"That was quick," she whispered, her voice a thread of sound in the shadows. She closed her eyes and then focused on Seb's face. "Did you get the matches?"

He waved his hand in an abrupt dismissal and growled something succinct and French, which Monty wasn't quick enough to catch.

"What did you say?" She rubbed her hand across her forehead and realized the skin of her palm prickled and tingled as if it had been slapped.

"Are you all right?" His accent roughened with concern. "You were supposed to sit on the step and wait for me. Why did you start down the stairs in this darkness?"

Start down the stairs? Is that what she had done? "I don't know," she said.

"Did something frighten you?"

She tried to focus her memory on the moments immediately preceding her fall. "I don't know," she repeated slowly. "It all happened very fast. I was standing at the top of the stairs and thinking about..." What *had* she been thinking about? Creepy crawlies. Yes, that was it. "I was thinking about 'Frère Jacques'."

"I thought you were an only child."

"No, no." She shook her head and immediately wished she hadn't. "I mean, yes, I am an only child. I was talking about the song."

He cleared his throat and then laid his palm against her forehead, his concern flowing into her like a healing salve. Closing her eyes, she shut out the haloed beam of the flashlight and tried to recall just what had happened. "I thought...I imagined...someone else was here. It felt as if I were...as if someone... pushed me."

His hesitation quivered in the silence. "We are alone in the tunnel," he said tightly. "And *I* did not push you."

Until that moment, she hadn't considered that his hand could have been at her back or that he was the only other person in the tunnel. Of course, until that moment she hadn't been clearheaded enough to consider much of anything. She waited for fear to rise like a flash flood inside her, but beneath his touch she felt only the faint but flourishing spark of desire. "Did you get the matches?" she asked.

For an instant, he was very still, then his movements jostled her. In the space of a very few heartbeats, he extended his open palm to the revealing glow of the flashlight and Monty saw the small box of matches that had, indeed, been on the table beside her bed. Which meant nothing... or everything.

"I did not push you," he said again. "Are you certain this was not another... accident?"

She wasn't absolutely certain of anything... except that the matches weren't an unbreakable alibi, and that—conversely—she felt safe and protected by his nearness. "I don't know. Maybe I did get too close to the edge of the top stair. I remember stomping my feet." She grimaced as she shifted positions and pressed her palm against the wall. "I guess I grabbed the railing when I first started to fall, and that's how I kept from tumbling all the way to the bottom."

He shone the flashlight beam over the rough-hewn rail that extended from the top of the narrow stairwell into the darkness several feet below. "You could have been killed."

The words grew and became a nauseating chant. *The Last Carlisle Heir... Will Die... Will Die...*

But before the fear could manifest itself as a shiver, Sebastian gathered her into his arms and held her tightly against the solid, steady beating of his heart. She rested her hands on his chest and absorbed the warm, rough texture of his shirt. His lips grazed the crown of her head and she relaxed into his embrace. Sebastian de Vergille would not harm her.

"I will take you back to your room," he whispered at her temple. "You have had enough adventure for tonight."

She gave a decidedly limp nod and realized, on some vague plane, that her entire body was too tranquil in the aftermath of the fall to do more. But when he stood and pulled her up with him, bringing her body into full contact with his, the tranquillity vanished in a wave of sensual shock.

Her soft gasp of discovery echoed in the tunnel, like the wind-ruffled pages of an open book. For a moment, she thought perhaps Seb hadn't heard or had misinterpreted the sound. He simply stood with his hands wrapped around her shoulders, holding her as if she were a will-o'-the-wisp, as still as the statues that adorned the château. And then, with fragmented and shaken courage, Monty lifted her chin and looked into his dark eyes.

The flashlight lay at their feet, its light pooled and muted, casting Seb's face in docile shadows, tracing the smoky line of his eyebrows and the shining richness of his dark hair. Her pulse rate went from slow idle to overdrive in a heartbeat, and her body heat climbed from a low-grade fever to a dangerous high. She wondered if he could feel the heat radiating from her, hear the thunderous sound of her heart racing in the urgent silence. She wanted him to kiss her, to take advantage of her here in the intimacy of the secret passageway, but the only persuasion she could muster was to run the tip of her tongue along the inside edge of her lip.

His hands slid from her shoulders, gradually moving down her arms until he captured her fingers and raised them to his lips, where he kissed each fingertip in turn with tender and unhurried care.

Monty's head spun as she watched his lips move across her hand with a touch as foreign and seductive as the liquid glow that was spilling over inside her. "Please tell me it's time to swoon," she whispered.

"It's time I behaved as a gentleman and took you back to your room." He rubbed his thumbs in sensual circles across her palms, but when he touched the scraped skin Monty winced and he immediately stepped back.

"What is this?" He cupped her palm and looked at the reddened and angry scratches. "You are hurt."

The tension was suddenly overwhelming, and Monty tried to tug her hand from his grasp. "I'm fine," she said in a tone still thready and breathlessly thin. "I think maybe I caught a splinter or two when I fell, that's all."

He bent his head and pressed his lips lightly against her skin, sending a jumble of sensual messages spiraling up her arm. *"Je regrette,"* he whispered into her hand. "I should never have left you alone."

"I might have fallen even if you'd been here, Seb." It had to have been an accident. She had been leaning forward at the top of the stairs, debating whether to sit down or remain standing in the dark. It would have been easy to lose her footing. And the memory of pressure, the feel of that hand on her back? Imagination. Aunt Jo's voodoo at work every time the lights went out.

With a minimum of movement, he retrieved the flashlight and placed it in her uninjured hand. "You're the guiding light this time," he said. "If we lose our way, it will be your responsibility." Then he scooped her up and into his arms, and walking at a sideways angle, he carried her through the tunnel.

Keeping the flashlight beam spotlighted on the path ahead, Monty looped her free hand behind his neck and felt an odd thrill as her fingers nestled into the thick pleat of hair at his nape. "Your hair is long for a man," she said. "Are you rebelling against convention or just making a statement?"

He didn't break his stride, but his grip on her tightened for a moment. "I have made a vow not to cut my hair until I have restored my heritage."

"Are you serious?"

"Why does that surprise you, *mademoiselle?* Have you never made a promise which you were honor bound to fulfill?"

Monty couldn't think of any promise she had ever made that involved her sense of honor. Bets, yes. She always honored her wagers, even the dumb ones. But promises? She didn't think so.

"Sebastian..." She wrapped a strand of his hair around her little finger and enjoyed the heavy texture as it twined about her knuckle. "What if someone...someone special...asked you to cut your hair? Would you do it? Even if you hadn't found the chalice?"

He walked steadily, passing the entrance to the north tower and moving through the passageway with ease. Monty thought he probably could have navigated just as effortlessly without the light she kept fixed on the tunnel ahead. They reached the half-opened secret entrance to her bedchamber, and she reined in her impatience to hear his answer as he pushed past the opening and carried her to the bed. Employing the flashlight as a brace, she fastened her arms firmly around his neck and decided she wasn't letting go until she'd gotten an answer to her question. And maybe, too, the kiss he'd denied her in the tunnel.

"Tell the truth, Sebastian," she said as he lowered her body to the plush contours of the mattress. "Would you break your vow for a woman?"

His gaze settled into hers like the velvet blanket of an approaching storm in a summer sky. For long, breathless leaps of time, he held her motionless and anticipating, with the intensity of his eyes and the sexy curve of his lower lip. And then, he caressed her with a slow smile. "Not even for you, *ma fleur.*"

She smoothed a strand of his hair with her fingertip, keeping her arms securely fastened around him. "What if I asked you very nicely?"

"Non." He clasped his hands over hers and firmly pulled her arms from around his neck, pinning her between his forbidding presence and the too-forgiving mattress. *"Non, mademoiselle.* Not even if you invited me into your bed." Then, as if he could restrain the desire no longer, he leaned in and captured her parted lips.

From the first moment, his kiss owned her. In an instant, her normally stubborn will became malleable, her body accepting and pliable under the scintillating pressure of his mouth. She was accustomed to enjoying life, and this exhilarating sensation was definitely on her updated list of pleasures to be savored. With a soft mewling sound, she wriggled into the folds of the downy comforter and relaxed her grip on the flashlight, allowing it to roll from her grasp.

It landed somewhere amid the bed covers and muffled what little light had been provided. But Monty greeted the shadows, granting the enveloping dusk a sensual welcome. With Seb's kiss, she had illumination enough to last through a dozen nights. His tongue glided across the soft, supple lining of her lips and a burning, liquid ache of desire smothered what few inhibitions she had left after her fall. A sharp, scintillating need twined through her, and she allowed her hands the freedom to touch and explore the vast, muscular region of his shoulders.

The brush of his hair against her fingertips reminded her of his vow. He had made a vow, a promise to himself. She admired that, thought it demonstrated purpose and determination and an attractive depth of character. Was that true? Sebastian seemed like the kind of man who would make such a vow, who would honor his heritage in such a manner. On the other hand, he could have made up the story just as easily. Not that she cared either way. She liked the feel of his hair, liked the way his body was tightly muscled beneath her hands. At the moment, she couldn't think of a thing about Sebastian she didn't like. He was mysterious, provocative and undoubtedly dangerous. How could she resist such a temptation? Why would she?

But when he pulled back from the kiss, drawing apart from the embrace, she felt a strange emptiness take his place. And of all things, she was afraid of emptiness. "Come back," she whispered, her fingers sliding to his shoulders to give a persuasive massage. "The adventure can't be over yet."

"*Mademoiselle,* you took a bad fall. You should rest and recover." He was half standing, half leaning across the mattress, and Monty made a last effort to draw him down beside her. But as her grip tightened on his taut biceps, he winced.

She was immediately concerned. "What's wrong with your arm?"

He shook his head and pulled free of her touch. "It is nothing. A bruise. Nothing."

A bruise. Of course. He'd said he had been in the hall, had bumped against the angel, had knocked it over. Didn't that prove that the accident had been just that . . . an accident? "And what about the scrape on your arm, Seb? The scrape I saw on that same arm this morning in the garden. Are you accident-prone or is that, too, a result of our brush with the angel?"

The silence swirled in her ears, and his tension pressed her back against the pillows. For a moment, she thought he would turn and disappear into the shadows, but instead he leaned over her and in the dusk she saw him smile.

"What are you asking, *ma fleur?* Are you, at last, afraid of me?"

Her heart jammed against her rib cage and then fluttered in helpless denial. "I'm not afraid of anything," she reminded him with brazen indifference to the wild beating of her pulse and the undeniable tremor in her throat.

"Except spiders." His breath was warm on her face as he placed both hands flat on either side of her shoulders and shifted his weight from the floor to the mattress. In a moment, he was kneeling above her and she searched futilely for the fear she knew she ought to be feeling instead of this wild and raging excitement. "You are afraid of spiders," he repeated. "And you are afraid of me."

He swooped down and fastened a second burning caress onto her lips, a kiss meant to prove his point, but which only sealed the attraction that flared, hot and desperately sexual, between them. And there, suddenly, she found the fear. She was afraid. Deeply afraid that he could be pretending, could be seducing her for reasons beyond desire, could well be telling her a lie with his kisses.

In determination to hold him until she knew the truth, she grasped the fabric of his shirt and twisted it in her fists. But his kiss remained just as devastatingly mysterious, and the only truth she discovered was that he was no more eager than she to end the torturous embrace. When he settled his body over hers, pressing her down into the rumpled bed covers and into the contours of the mattress beneath, her hands were captured in the folds of his shirt, locked between his hard, muscled weight and the knowledge that she didn't want to be released.

As his chest pressed against hers, her nipples peaked and her breasts grew heavy with a perilous melting warmth. Somehow, she managed to slip out of her shoes, and then her feet were free to nuzzle the rough cloth that covered his calves. He shuddered beneath her touch and she chased the sensation as far up his leg as her toes could reach, which wasn't nearly far enough. Leaving her lips blushing with his imprint, he buried her senses in a snowdrift of quick sipping kisses which he trailed across her cheek to her earlobe and down the smooth slope of her neck to the pulsing hollows of her throat.

And he'd said she had had enough adventure for one night. The man was a veritable steamroller of adventure. From every angle, he was leading her into new territory and showing no hesitation in taking full advantage of her weakened condition.

Weakened? Ha! She felt wonderful. Her head spun, she felt so good. Even telling herself that "nice girls" didn't allow such latitude on a first date didn't make any difference. Her body merely countered the platitude with a dozen delicate shivers of delight. She had never before met a man like Sebastian.... A man who had immediately and completely commanded her attention ... A man who kissed her as if he meant it ... A man who dared her in subtle and not so subtle ways ... A man she trusted instinctively, without knowing why, or even if, she should ... And best of all, a man who thought she was a secretary.

His weight shifted. His hand trailed over her stomach and settled on her breast, and she knew the time had come either to swoon or take a stand. Playing with fire was one thing, deliberately creating an inferno was quite another. Reluctantly, she let go of the death grip she had on his shirt, but before she could call a halt to his progress he rolled quickly off the bed and onto his feet.

Monty frowned in confusion. Sure, she'd intended to stop him, but she'd meant to do it gradually, ease away from the embrace, linger over a couple of "cooling down" kisses. She certainly hadn't meant for Sebastian to jump out of her arms and off the bed. As she opened her lips to voice a protest, he clapped his hand across her mouth and motioned her to silence. In the ensuing stillness, she heard a faint scratching sound and turned her head, with Seb's hand still covering her mouth, toward the far door, the door leading to Eve's bedchamber.

The sound came again and Monty nodded, indicating to Seb that she heard and understood the need for quiet. The last thing she wanted was for Eve to walk through that door and find her locked in an embrace with the gardener...or anyone else for that matter. Sebastian probably wasn't eager to meet the woman he believed to be his employer under these circumstances, either. Monty pushed upright on the bed and turned to ask Sebastian if he thought he ought to leave, but he was already halfway across the room and barely visible in the shadows.

"Seb?" she whispered.

He stopped, turned, and with matchless charm brought his heels together and executed his neat anything-but-subservient bow. She could see well enough to detect the rueful humor in his expression, too. No doubt, in another lifetime, Sebastian de Vergille had been the king of France. Her lips curved with a wry smile as she watched him slip from sight through the opening in the wall and into the tunnel beyond. Soundlessly, the opening disappeared and the wall again appeared seamless and complete. Monty decided she was going to examine that wall very closely tomorrow in the bright light of day.

The scratching noise became a distinct tapping on the connecting door, and Monty slid down beneath the covers and pulled them over her head. She stretched out, hoping Eve would look in and then go back to her own bed, convinced her employer was sound asleep.

Beneath the bulky comforter, Monty bumped something with her foot and then heard a loud metallic thump as the "something" hit the floor and rolled. The flashlight. Sebastian had forgotten the flashlight, and now it was rolling toward the door on which Eve was knocking.

The latch clicked and the door eased open. "Miss Carlisle?" Eve's whisper was underlined by the slow *ker-clunk, ker-clunk, ker-clunk* noise of the rolling flashlight. "Miss Carlisle? I thought I heard something. Are you all right?"

Monty pushed back the covers, sat up, and peered across the room at her granny-gowned secretary. The flashlight beam spooled in telltale circles as it traveled unerringly toward the door. Obviously, some explanation would have to be offered. She wondered what it might be as she waited for the incriminating *ker-clunk, ker-clunk* to tumble to a halt at Eve's house-slippered feet.

"Miss C-C-Carlisle?"

"Come in, Eve," Monty said. "Are you having trouble sleeping tonight?"

"A little." Eve's nervousness crept into the room like a cat on the prowl, and Monty wondered if she'd done something to intimidate the woman or if Eve was just naturally timid. "Wh-what's this?" Eve bent at the waist to pick up the flashlight. She held it loosely between her fingers as she straightened. "Where did you find a flashlight?"

"Under the bed."

Eve's mouth dropped open in a small O. "Really? I wouldn't have thought to look there."

"That's because you're afraid there might be a ghost under it." Monty reached back and made a show of plumping the pillow. "Live dangerously, Eve. Look under your bed."

"All right...if you think I should. Here." She came forward, turning off the flashlight's beam as she reached the far side of the bed. When Monty didn't lean across to take it, Eve dropped the flashlight onto the bed covers. "Were you asleep? I did think I heard a noise."

"I must have been snoring." Monty punched the pillow once more and stuffed it behind her back. "Unless there's a ghost under *my* bed."

Eve's chin dipped to her chest like a scolded child. "I'm sorry," she said. "I shouldn't have bothered you."

Monty was instantly contrite. "You were merely concerned. I shouldn't have teased you about the ghosts. You know I have a warped sense of humor."

"Oh, no, you're not warped. I take everything too seriously, that's all."

At this rate, an exchange of apologies could go on forever. "In all fairness to you, Castle Carlisle isn't exactly fun city."

"You seem to be having a good time."

She was, Monty realized. So far, her exile had been full of surprises. And the possibility for more adventure and a bit of romance was even now making his way through the secret passageway. Monty kept her pleasure to herself and shared only a little shrug with her secretary. "You know me. Just trying to make the best of the situation."

"Are you sorry you made that bet with Stanton Grainger?" Eve plucked nervously at the covers on Monty's bed. "You might never have had to come here if it wasn't for that bet."

"Aunt Jo would have found some excuse to lock me away somewhere until my birthday. I'm sure that if she could have thought of a way to burn every spinning wheel in the world, she'd have done that, too."

"Spinning wheel?" Eve sounded completely baffled, and Monty hoped the next secretary would be better able to think on her feet.

"The legend of Sleeping Beauty," Monty explained. "On her sixteenth birthday, she was lured to the tower and pricked her finger on the spindle of a spinning wheel. She slept for a hundred years until Alec Baldwin awakened her with a kiss.''

''Alec Baldwin?''

Monty nodded solemnly. ''I suppose there are some women who will claim it was actually Kevin Costner, but I personally like Alec in the role of Prince Charming.''

Eve drew a tiny circle on the comforter with her fingertip. ''What role would you cast Sebastian in?''

Obviously, Eve was paying more attention than Monty had thought. She frowned as if she had to consider the possibilities. ''A pirate, maybe. Or a highwayman. He might even pass as a swashbuckling podiatrist.''

Eve didn't laugh. She didn't even look up as she drew a few more circles in the plush folds of the comforter. ''I kind of had the idea you might try to cast him as your very own Prince Charming.''

Well, well, well, Monty thought. Behind that flannel-gown facade and nervous demeanor lurked a few unexpected observations. ''*My* Prince Charming?'' Monty managed a laugh and an evasive answer. ''Now, that's an interesting possibility.''

Eve's head jerked up. ''But he's a gardener.''

''And I'm a secretary. What could be more perfect?''

''What will happen when he finds out who you really are? You don't know anything about him, Miss Carlisle. I wish you wouldn't get involved.''

Monty shed the warning with an ease that came from years of practice. "I can handle Sebastian," she said.

Eve nodded as if she had expected to be ignored. "I hope so, because he's a dangerous man."

"Maybe that's why I find him so attractive. I plan to spend as much time as possible with him while I'm in exile." As another protest loomed on the horizon, Monty decided to head it off at the pass with another round of worry. "In fact, in the morning, I want you to send us to Paris on an errand."

"Errand?" The single word packed a fortune in disapproval. "What kind of an errand?"

Monty shrugged, pleased with her inspiration. "It doesn't matter. You'll think of something."

"But you shouldn't be running all over Paris with . . . with him."

"Really? Why not?"

"Well, because. . . It isn't. . . I mean, he's only the. . ." Eve stumbled over the protest. "It just isn't a good idea."

With a slight arching of her brow, Monty disagreed. "I think it's a great idea."

"Edwin will be furious."

"Uncle Edwin has no say in the matter. I'm in exile because he wanted to handle things his way. How I choose to entertain myself while I'm in exile is none of his concern."

"I'll go to Paris with you. There's no need to involve the gardener."

Monty laughed to keep from getting irritated. "I appreciate your willingness to sacrifice yourself, Eve, but that won't be necessary."

"But Edwin told me..." Her sentence trailed into abject silence.

"I'm sure Edwin gave you all kinds of instructions. And now I'm giving you permission to ignore those instructions and enjoy your vacation. Remember? We agreed on the trip over here. You would masquerade as me and do the things you like to do. I would masquerade as you and do what I want. So tomorrow while I'm gone, go shopping in the village or read one of those books you always seem to have tucked under your arm. Take a walk. But whatever you do, don't spend any time worrying about me."

Eve did not look convinced. "You don't know anything about him, Miss Carlisle."

She did. She knew everything of importance. With a nod, she resumed the role of employer and dismissed her employee. "Good night, Eve. I'm sure you'll be able to sleep now."

For a moment, Monty thought there would be more argument, but Eve's shoulders drooped with resignation and then lifted as if she were relieved to be rid of the responsibility. "Good night, then. I won't bother you any longer."

As Eve turned and shuffled to the doorway, Monty experienced a pang of remorse. "I appreciate your concern," she said. "I hope I didn't sound ungrateful."

Eve glanced briefly over her shoulder. "Apology accepted."

Apology? That hadn't been an apology. But as Eve left the room and quietly closed the door behind her, Monty decided the woman was entitled to infer any meaning she chose. What difference did it make? Tomorrow, Montgomery Carlisle, in the role of mild-mannered secretary Eve O'Halloran, would convince Seb to take her into Paris. She would see the city from a new perspective, Seb's perspective. They would have lunch in a sidewalk café, perhaps. Or maybe he would know of a secluded hideaway in the city, a place she would never have chanced upon on her own. The thought was enchanting, exciting, delightful.

A day in Paris with a man whose kisses burned holes in her soul—what more could she ask for?

She tucked her scraped palm beneath her cheek and settled her head on the pillows. All she had to do now was to come up with a believable excuse for the trip. Maybe being given an errand to run really was her best bet. Eve, posing as Monty, would ask Sebastian to go into Paris and buy...oh, something or other. The Mona Lisa, maybe, or some other outlandish item. It was all a matter of planning—careful planning.

She pulled the covers over her head and promptly fell asleep.

IN THE TUNNEL, Seb lit the candles and tucked the matches back inside his pocket. He had been careless tonight—inexcusably careless. What would he have said if Mademoiselle O'Halloran had discovered his presence in Montgomery's room? Or, even worse, what if she had discovered the passageway herself? Too many people already knew of its existence. Too many knew the truth about his search. And he was wholly responsible for adding one more.

Montgomery Carlisle. How could he have guessed her lips would taste so sweet? He had believed ... what? That he could dance with fire and not be burned? Too true. And he couldn't say he hadn't been warned. Charlotte had tried to tell him, counseled him to reconsider. And Charlotte didn't know the half of it.

He lifted the flickering light and looked down. The staircase yawned like an empty grave, and he clenched his jaw. The wood railing was rough and weathered, but it had saved her life.

Someone pushed me.

Turning abruptly, Sebastian moved away from the stairs and approached the north tunnel. Another accident, he thought. Just as Charlotte had predicted. But Monty hadn't been scared. Which only meant she was either very foolish or very naive, to be so unconcerned.

And he was very stupid to admire her courage. Very stupid, indeed.

Chapter Six

"And then I want you to go to Shakespeare & Company and pick up a book for me." Eve looked up from the list she was holding in her hand. "Are you familiar with the bookstore I mean?"

Sebastian nodded. "On Rue de la Bûcherie. I have been there before."

"Good." Eve handed the list to Monty. "Ask for Thomas. I spoke with him on the telephone and he's holding the book for me. I've written down the title for you, but make sure he gives you the English version."

Monty was impressed. Eve was really getting into the role of Montgomery Carlisle, American heiress incognito. From the moment they sat down at the long table in the massive, semimodernized kitchen with their breakfast croissants and coffee, Eve had been giving instructions as if she were queen for a day.

"Is that all?" Monty asked in her best I-aim-to-please voice, as she checked over the impressive list of errands. "Are you sure there isn't something you forgot to put down?"

Uncertainty flickered in Eve's blue eyes. "But you said—"

"I said I didn't mind." Monty hurried to interrupt. "And I meant it. As long as Seb can find the shops and act as translator, I'm happy to have a day in the city."

Eve looked relieved. "That's good, then. But please be very careful. I'd feel just awful if anything happened to you."

"What could happen?" Charlotte leaned back in her chair and sipped from her coffee cup, as if she were a woman of leisure who had nothing better to do. "People go to Paris every day. Other than spending too much money and eating too much, what could happen?"

"An accident or something," Eve said with an edge of anxiety. "I worry about that sort of thing, that's all."

"Waste of good time, worry is." Charlotte placed her cup on the table and measured each of her listeners in turn. "Nothin' was ever accomplished by worrying about it."

"Around here nothing is accomplished, period." Eve's tone was sharp and to the point.

Charlotte crossed her arms at her ample bosom. "Are you talkin' to me, *mademoiselle?*"

Monty could see this getting nasty fast. "Miss Carlisle?" she said with a big smile. "Would you go over the list with me one more time before Seb and I leave? Just to refresh my memory about what I'm supposed to get for you?"

"Certainly." Eve pushed to her feet in a quick and uncharacteristic show of annoyance. "Let's go upstairs."

As they walked from the kitchen and up the narrow servants' stairway to the great hall, Eve grabbed Monty's arm. "Did I do okay?" she whispered. "I was trying to act like you."

No doubt she meant that as the most sincere compliment, Monty thought. "You were terrific," she said. "I was absolutely convinced you were me."

Eve laughed. "Oh, I wasn't that good."

Monty hadn't realized she set such a high standard. She stuffed the note into the pocket of her jeans. "Well, Sebastian believed you and that's all I wanted in the first place. Now, promise me you'll do something nice for yourself while I'm gone."

A smile brightened Eve's whole demeanor. "I'm planning to do just that."

"Good. You can tell me all about it tonight when I get back."

"And you'll be extra careful?"

Monty held up her hand, palm facing out. "As careful as anyone can be in a rental car in a foreign country, driving at speeds exceeding all common sense."

But when she walked outside a little while later, there was a sleek-looking motorcycle parked where the rental car should have been. Sebastian was waiting beside the bike with helmet in hand and a certain smugness tucked in at the corners of his mouth. He hadn't changed clothes since breakfast, but suddenly the black jeans and white T-shirt took on a whole new dimension, lending him a dangerous bad-boy appearance. With his shoulder-length hair swept back and fastened loosely at his nape and with the black leather jacket slung carelessly across his shoulders, he was perilously attractive.

Her heart skipped a beat, and then another, as she approached and circled the motorcycle. "Moto Guzzi," she said, stealing a little of his smugness for her own. "Nice bike."

"Thank you. Want to ride with me...or do you prefer to follow in the car?"

With a hoydenish toss of her head, she faced him across the cycle. "What kind of question is that?" She took the helmet from him and pulled it on, smoothly tucking in any wayward strands of chestnut hair. "Remember me? Fearless Fiona?" She gave him a fabulous smile. "Can I drive?"

His eyebrows arched in moderate surprise. "You've ridden motorcycles before?"

"I can handle this one."

"You have experience?"

She lifted her shoulder in a cool, little shrug. "Experience is overrated."

"So is innocence, but neither is a good substitute for the other."

The uncompromising curve of his smile set the blood pumping excitedly through her veins, and the sensation was as unsettling as it was unfamiliar. Monty decided she liked the smile, the sensation, and the man . . . a lot.

"You should first practice on something with a little less power, before you ride into the sunset on this machine." Seb reached for a second helmet which was strapped on the rear passenger seat and fitted it over his own dark hair. His long fingers were covered by gloves that were as black as the jacket, but looked as soft and malleable as rich, dark earth. She watched, fascinated by the supple ripple of the leather as he tightened the straps of his helmet.

"The helmets are equipped with a two-way radio," he said. "So you don't have to fall off the bike to get my attention. You make adjustments to the sound here." He demonstrated with a touch to her helmet.

As she settled the visor in place and set the chin strap, he straddled the bike and held his hand out to assist her. "Get on, Fiona."

"That's Fearless to you, Monsieur de Vergille. And don't think you've heard the last of this. What I may lack in experience, I make up for in determination." Placing her hand in his gloved one, she swung her leg up and over the saddle seat and settled in behind him. Immediately, his body heat flowed through her like a sultry tropic breeze, making her fully and physically aware of his proximity, of the lean curvature of his back, the smooth firmness of his hips and the latent strength in his shoulders.

With a glance over his shoulder to check her position, he righted the bike and kicked the brace out of the way. Monty slid into his backside, and her arms wrapped around his waist as her knees squeezed against his thighs. He started the engine with practiced efficiency, and the powerful motor throbbed to vibrating life beneath her.

In an exhilarating burst of acceleration, Seb drove away from the château and Monty laughed aloud as the bike picked up speed. The wind whipped around her, and she plastered herself to the angle of Sebastian's body as the thrill of new experience mingled with her innocent awareness of the man who offered it.

SHE FELT WARM and feminine wrapped around him, her hands clasped at his waist, her knees clamped against his thighs. Her excitement was almost tangible—unmistakable in the throaty laughter he heard at infrequent intervals, evident when she leaned into the turns with him, manifest in the way she trembled with each new burst of speed.

"Are you enjoying the ride?" he asked.

Her answer came through the earpiece in his helmet, a bit scratchy but plump with her pleasure. "This is great! I'm buying one of these babies at the first opportunity." There was a pause and then her voice came through the earpiece again, graceful and enticing. "Could I persuade you to sell yours, perhaps?"

At that moment, he would have given her the bike, freely and with no strings attached, if she hadn't been Montgomery Carlisle. But she was Josiah Carlisle's heir. That undeniable fact could not be changed, and he would do well to remember it, too. "A man doesn't part with his Moto Guzzi," he said. "Not even at the request of such a beautiful woman as you, *mademoiselle.*"

"The offer stands...in case you want to think it over."

He had been doing a great deal of thinking since the night before. The memory of her ashen face had followed him into shadowy dreams of dark tunnels and bloodred rubies. Her accident on the stairs had scared him, and when she had said someone pushed her, he thought his heart had stopped right there and then. She must have been mistaken, must have taken that step forward without realizing how close she was to the edge of the stair. It had to have been an accident. No one else could have been there. And in fact, she hadn't been hurt.

But she might have been. A fall like that could have broken her neck. Would have, in all likelihood, if she hadn't had the presence of mind to grab the rail and save herself.

He kept coming back to that. She hadn't fallen—at least not far—and outside of a scraped hand, there was no evidence to back up her claim. Except her pallor, which he had seen even in the uncertain glow of the flashlight. A pallor that had sent a wave of distress careening through his soul. He had thought she was dead, had lived an eternity in the moments before discovering she wasn't hurt, had died a little when he thought she was pointing an accusing finger at him.

But then, quickly, she had admitted it was an accident, that she must have taken a misstep. All of which added up to nothing more than an uneasy feeling that she could be manipulating him just as easily as he believed he was manipulating her.

It could hardly have been more obvious to him that the trip today was a setup, choreographed by Monty for what purpose he could only guess. And his guess was that Montgomery Carlisle was looking for a diversion. Perhaps she hadn't as yet bedded a Frenchman. Or maybe it was the length of his hair, or even his position as her gardener that was the attraction. Whatever her motive, this daring and beautiful woman, this lover of new experiences, was playing with him.

At least . . . she thought she was.

"DID YOU HAVE SUCCESS?" Sebastian asked when Monty approached the motorcycle after having been inside a small salon on Rue du Faubourg St.-Honoré.

She lifted a shopping bag in answer, indicating that the requested hair clip was now in the bag. "That's everything on our errand list except the book at Shakespeare & Company."

Seb slid forward on the seat, and Monty climbed on behind him. "May we stop for *déjeuner?*" he asked.

"You're the guide. If you're hungry, by all means, let's get some lunch." She pulled on the helmet before slipping her arms around his waist.

He half turned toward her. "Do you have a favorite café?"

She had dined often in the most famous of Paris restaurants, was even known to a discerning maître d' or two, but cafés weren't normally included on her itinerary. "I don't know the city well enough to suggest one. You choose."

He barely took a moment to consider. "I'll take you to my favorite bistro."

Perfect, Monty thought. His favorite café wasn't likely to be a place where she might be recognized. She tightened her hold on his waist because she liked the feel of the leather jacket beneath her hands. The body beneath the jacket wasn't bad, either. "Is it nearby?"

"Not far." He started the motorcycle, looked for an opening in traffic and pulled into the flow.

From the back of the bike, Monty enjoyed a view of Paris she'd never before had the opportunity to see. Her past visits to this magnificent city had been charted and planned down to the last minute, and she had been chauffeured from point to point. Under Aunt Jo's neurotic eye and Edwin's protective thumb, she had hardly been allowed to enjoy the major tourist attractions. She'd been surprised that she and Eve had been permitted to drive the rental car to the château upon their arrival in France. Of course, as Edwin liked to remind her, she was "hiding out." No one was supposed to know she was even in the country. What a dilemma her uncle must have had when he realized the only way for her to get from Point *A*, Charles de Gaulle airport, to Point *B*, Château Carlisle, with any anonymity was to forgo a chauffeur and allow her to drive a rental car. She'd have to remember to goad him a bit about that.

And of course she'd take great delight in telling him about this jaunt. Wouldn't she love for him to see her now? On the back of a motorcycle, moving through the back streets of Paris, chauffeured by a gardener in black leather, clinging to him as if she were the president of his fan club? A man of mystery, too. What would Edwin make of that?

"Notre-Dame." Sebastian's voice came through the earpiece and recalled her to the moment. She looked up and recognized the great cathedral and the Eiffel Tower in the distance. The architectural treasures of Paris were breathtaking from any angle, in any weather, and she couldn't keep from drawing a deep, appreciative breath.

"It is a beautiful city," she said. "Do you spend much time here?"

"I keep an apartment near the bistro where we will have lunch. I am often in Paris."

"Are you a gardener when you're here?"

His laugh was a soft caress within the confines of her helmet. "I am a gardener even when I am in Texas, *mademoiselle.* It is my profession."

Gardening suddenly took on new dimensions in Monty's mind. "Wait a minute," she said. "Did you say you've been to Texas?"

"Yes, ma'am," he drawled in a pretty good imitation of a man who lived right near the Rio Grande. "I lived there for several years when I was a youth."

No wonder he spoke such fluent and idiomatic English. "You might have told me before now, Sebastian."

"You never asked."

True enough. What with midnight meanderings through the château, the state of Texas had never crossed her mind. "Not fair, Seb. How could I have guessed you were a foreign exchange student?"

"I wasn't. My mother is American. I have dual citizenship."

That intrigued her even more, although she didn't know how her interest in Sebastian could get any more intense. "Lucky you," was all she could think to say.

Seb braked, and the motorcycle glided easily into a tiny parking spot just visible between the uneven row of parked cars. Monty pulled off her helmet and shook the stiffness from her hair, fluffing it out and away from her scalp.

"I hope it doesn't rain on us during the trip back this afternoon." Sebastian moved to get off the bike and squinted at the patch of sky visible overhead. "You might not like riding wet."

Monty looked up. The air held a scent of rain, and the sky had grown heavy with ponderous clouds. She swung her leg over the seat and reached for his hand to steady herself. "With you, Sebastian, I'm sure riding wet would be quite an adventure."

His eyes met hers, and like a flash fire, sexual awareness burned her senses and bled into her cheeks. Her throat felt suddenly tight and dry, and she made a valiant effort to moisten her lips with her tongue. She almost never blushed, she wasn't easily embarrassed, but something about Sebastian was so...seductive. And she didn't even know if he meant to seduce her— or even if he wanted to do so.

He kept her fingers enclosed within his gloved fist, and the touch of the leather against her skin felt deliciously sensual. When his lips formed a smoothly alluring curve, her heart did a dropkick and fluttered halfway between heaven and hell. She swallowed hard. "I, uh, meant to say riding in the rain would be an adventure."

"I am your adventure, *mademoiselle*. Enjoy me, as I am enjoying you."

Her poor heart gave a helpless little shudder and then leapt into passionate approval of his sentiment. Common sense kept the rhythmic pounding of her pulse from quivering in her voice and betraying her silly heart as she slowly withdrew her hand from his and returned his smile with equanimity. "If there's an ounce of Texan in you, I'll eat a ten-gallon hat."

"Let's see what's on the menu first. You may find an entrée that is more appealing." He stripped off the gloves and tucked them into his jacket pocket as he moved forward and pulled open a heavy wooden door. "This establishment is not as old nor as famous as others in the city, but Madame Rozzell is a fabulous cook."

Monty's mouth was watering already.

Inside, the bistro was long and narrow, full of glistening dark wood and row upon row of glasses. It smelled of good wine and old smoke, and hummed with the sound of savored conversations. A man wearing a blue beret stood at the bar, staring into a glass of dark red wine. Beside him, a woman in a saffron-colored sweater sipped from a thick-rimmed coffee mug. A mirror behind the bar reflected everything from the single potted plant at the entrance to the rosy stain on Monty's cheeks. Automatically, she lifted her hand to rub away the color and decided that motorcycling had to be healthy. Look what a bit of fresh air had done for her.

From the back of the room, a second woman came forward, rubbing her hands on the stained skirt of her apron and carrying with her the pungent aroma of the kitchen. She was small but robust, and her graying hair was curled and twisted into an abbreviated knot on top of her head. Catching sight of the newcomers, she began speaking to Seb in rapid-fire French.

Monty caught the gist of the conversation, enough to realize that her companion was no stranger to the neighborhood bar, that he was a welcomed and valued regular, although he hadn't been in recently. Using a few words, Seb managed to include her in his welcome, and the woman, Madame Rozzell, greeted her with a few words of enthusiastic if barely recognizable English. They were quickly bustled to a table and encouraged to order anything they desired from the menu chalked on a small blackboard on the wall.

As Madame Rozzell marched off to fix the café au lait that she insisted they have to drink, Monty tucked a strand of hair behind her ear and visually examined the man who sat across from her. Sebastian looked at home and easy here in this neighborhood bistro. His black jacket was unzipped and open, revealing a slice of white cotton and a small triangle of chest hair curling in the unbuttoned V of the shirt. A trickle of longing made a slow loop in her stomach as she stared at the wiry, dark swirls that just brushed the hollow of his throat.

"You look hungry," he said. "May I order for you, or would you rather have the ten-gallon hat?"

Monty tore her gaze from his chest and tried to remember the last time she'd felt so foolish about a man. Was it Seb's uniqueness or the idea that he didn't know her true identity? "If I thought they'd have Pick-a-Pepper sauce, I'd order the hat." She allowed her lips a careful and not overly foolish smile. "Please order something for me. Madame Rozzell's specialty."

He nodded and settled more comfortably—if that were possible—in the chair. "Tell me about being Montgomery Carlisle's secretary," he said.

"What's to tell? It isn't a terribly interesting job."

"Come now, *petite fleur*. You're being modest. Mademoiselle Carlisle is a fascinating woman. Why wouldn't working for her be fascinating as well?"

Monty shifted in her chair and tapped the table with an anxious fingertip. This subject made her uneasy. Or maybe it was the look in his eyes that set her nerves on edge. Monty frowned and forced herself to relax. Who was she kidding, anyway? Every move the man made disturbed one part or another of her anatomy. "What did you want to know about her, Sebastian?"

He shrugged. "Does she insist that you type very fast?"

A rueful smile edged onto her lips and into her eyes. "Well, I have to type about as fast as you have to trim the grass, Sebastian. Miss Carlisle is a very understanding employer."

"Really? She seems rather demanding."

"Oh, but she's incredibly patient."

"Hmm. I would have guessed her to be a trifle intolerant."

"Oh, no." Monty warmed to her own defense. "She's just accustomed to having her own way."

"Ah, she's spoiled."

"No." But that might be a hard point to sell. Monty settled for a slight concession. "Maybe a little, but she's very generous."

He nodded as if considering the charge. "And of course she is undeniably beautiful."

Monty faltered in midchallenge. "Oh," she said. "Well, yes, I suppose she is . . . if you like her type."

The light of laughter shone in his dark eyes. "I am surprised she hired you. She must realize how her beauty pales in comparison to yours."

Monty was suddenly glad he had a dual nationality. If the other half of his chromosomes had been French, too, she'd no doubt be on the floor, kissing his feet by this time. "Miss Carlisle isn't the jealous kind," was the best rejoinder she could come up with.

Madame Rozzell returned with two cups of coffee and set them, steaming and rich with milk, on the table in front of Seb. He thanked her and ordered a light lunch, which was altered several times to agree with Madame Rozzell's insistent suggestions. She glanced once at Monty and then informed Sebastian that his *amie* needed nourishment, not a "light lunch." He laughed and shrugged in reply. Obviously satisfied with that result, the proprietress left for the kitchen, leaving Seb to focus his attention again on Monty.

He ran his fingertip over the thick oatmeal-colored handle of one of the coffee mugs and smiled. "Are you jealous?"

"Of Madame Rozzell?" Monty laughed. "Yes. She can cook and she doesn't seem to have a bit of trouble putting you in your place."

Humor softened the smile. "I meant, are you jealous of Montgomery Carlisle?"

Immediately, her tension returned. "Why would I be jealous of her? You've just said her beauty pales next to mine."

"But she has money, power, everything a woman might desire at her fingertips."

"You're too intelligent to believe that wealth equals happiness, Seb."

He turned one of the mugs so that the handle faced her. "Are you telling me you wouldn't exchange places with her if you could?"

This was getting a little too personal, she thought. And a bit too close for comfort. "I'm only saying that Montgomery Carlisle would give every treasure she owns to know that she was loved for who she is and not for what she possesses." The declaration sounded emphatic and desperate, and Monty invented a smile to cover her embarrassment. "In my opinion, anyway."

He lifted his mug and blew gently at the heat spiraling upward in wisps of steam. "And so, would you or would you not trade places with her...if, of course, a trade of identities were possible?"

"No. No, I wouldn't."

As he drank from the mug, he regarded her thoughtfully and the tension inside her built to the point where she could hardly catch her breath. "You are an unusual woman, *ma fleur,* and if we were not in Madame Rozzell's bistro, I would kiss you."

Monty's throat tightened even more, and she did her best not to breathe in short revealing gasps. "I didn't think time and place made any difference to a Frenchman."

"That depends on what time and what place."

She met the challenge in his gaze. "Well," she said softly. "This is Paris."

The curve of his lips was tempting and altogether too sexy. "Ah, but you forget, I am also a Texan and it is time for lunch."

Her smile started slowly, but more than answered his. "I should have ordered the hat."

THE RAIN STARTED as they drove away from the bistro, and by the time they reached the *Rue de la Bûcherie,* the clouds opened to drench them in a chilling downpour. There was no place to park and Seb pulled the motorcycle to a stop in the street outside Shakespeare & Company. "You get the book," he said into the helmet's mouthpiece. "I will go around and return for you."

He slid far forward on the seat so she could bring her leg up and over and get off the bike. Still wearing the helmet, Monty ran between two parked cars and entered the bookstore. A horn bleated behind him and Seb moved forward with the traffic. As he came around the block a second time, he saw a parking space open up on the opposite side of the street. With some skillful maneuvering, he managed to backtrack and come up to the space just ahead of a small red sports car. He zipped into the space, narrowly cutting off the other car. The driver of the sports car honked the horn in a blast of irritation before revving the engine and screeching off.

A split second later, tires squealed in protest, followed by a resounding thud and the noise of shattering glass. Seb jerked around just in time to see a shiny black ball bounce across the rain-slick street toward him.

But it wasn't a plastic ball. With a nauseating twist of his stomach, he realized the object was a motorcycle helmet.

Chapter Seven

Despite the rain, a crowd gathered in front of the bookstore, surrounding and supporting Monty with collective concern. Expressions of distress and questions about the accident poured over her in waves of fluid French. She heard them, interpreted them, and yet was only vaguely aware of the confusion around her. She stood, her hips and hands pressed flat against the hood of a parked car, her arms trembling with the trauma of supporting her weight, buffeted by the well-meaning attempts of the people who were asking her over and over again if she were all right.

"I'm fine," she said in a voice that barely approached a whisper. "The car didn't hit me."

But if she hadn't heard the blare of a horn, hadn't looked up as she started across the street, hadn't seen the dark sedan racing toward her...

Thomas, the clerk from the bookstore, pushed through the crowd to reach her. "What happened? I looked out when I heard the squeal of the tires. I thought you'd been hit for sure."

His American voice was oddly soothing and she turned toward him, although she kept her body braced against the parked car. "I don't know what happened," she said. "I saw a dark sedan and then this. . . ." She looked at the little red car and its shattered windshield. "This car came barreling into the lane, right into the sedan's path. I thought they were going to crash." She had thought both vehicles were going to crash into her. "I . . . jumped back and . . ." Something pinched her memory. Something about the dark sedan. Something she couldn't quite catch hold of. "I . . . I don't remember what happened then."

"The helmet flew out of her hands," a bystander said. "It hit that car, then smashed into the windshield of this one."

"Yes," another witness confirmed. "The helmet bounced off the hood of the sedan and then into the windshield of the other. I saw it. I was standing right over there. I saw the whole thing."

"It's a wonder you weren't killed," Thomas said, and with those words, Monty's heart stopped.

Another accident. With a turn of her head, she found the motorcycle, parked and abandoned on the opposite side of the street. But Sebastian was nowhere in sight. His helmet lay on the seat in mute testimony to his absence, and a wave of fear and confusion swept over her.

And then, suddenly, he was beside her and the vague suspicion turned into utter relief. With a soft cry, she went into his arms and buried her face in the wet warmth of his embrace. He pulled her back into the doorway of the bookstore and draped his leather jacket around her shoulders, taking care to keep her safe and sheltered with his body.

"You're all right." His voice trembled on the words, shaped them into a thankful prayer, and she became aware of the tension in his arms.

She looked up and saw the anguish in his face, the distress in his stormy dark eyes. "Seb," she whispered. "I think someone meant to kill me."

He cupped the back of her head with his hand and drew her cheek to rest against his chest. He was wet from the rain and the heat from his body enclosed her like a steam bath. His heartbeat echoed reassuringly in her ear, strong and solid and very much alive. "Shh," he murmured against her hair. "You're safe now. Safe with me."

SEBASTIAN'S APARTMENT was larger than a hotel room, but not by much. Monty collapsed into a cushioned chair and felt as if she were home. The three-room flat would have fit twice over into a single bedroom of her California estate. The swimming pool at her home was easily three times as large. But at this moment, there was no comparison. The apartment won, hands down.

"You're feeling all right?" He placed his palm on her forehead as if there were a chance she'd developed a fever in the past five minutes. "Do you want something to drink? Juice? Wine? An antacid?"

Monty smiled, amused and comforted by his concern. Reaching up, she placed her hand over his and drew it gently away from her forehead. "I feel fine, just a bit tired. That's a normal reaction to this afternoon's accident, I suppose."

He knelt beside the chair, turning his hand until her fingers were intertwined with his. "No one was able to describe the other car except as you did, a dark sedan that sped away from the scene after causing the accident."

"It could have just...happened." The words sounded wistful, even in her own ears. "I mean, the two cars were both going too fast. It could have been a coincidence." The look in his eyes told her he didn't believe that any more than she did. "There was something about the sedan, something I keep trying to remember."

He squeezed her fingers and she gave him a wispy smile. "I keep thinking that if the driver of that red car hadn't honked his horn, I would have kept walking and—" A shiver did a slow crawl up her spine.

"But that is not what happened. You are here with me. You are safe. Nothing happened."

But something had happened, and they were both acutely aware of the fact. She drew a deep breath and forced her thoughts away from the dramatic. "Your spare helmet didn't come out so well."

"I died a thousand deaths when I saw it bouncing across the street."

Sincerity framed the words and his expression, and Monty believed him. It was strange, the way she felt about Sebastian. He was still so much a mystery to her, yet she trusted him with her whole heart, more than she had ever trusted another human being and with far less reason. She was thankful that he had handled the details of the incident, talked to the people who wanted endless information, dealt with the questions she didn't know how to answer. She was grateful for the tight grip of his hand over hers, for the sanctuary he offered.

And now, as she looked into his eyes, she felt emotions that both excited and frightened her. What was the tenuous bond that bound her to him? And how had it come into existence so quickly, so unexpectedly? And was it possible that he felt the same?

More questions she could not answer, didn't even want to think about. At the moment, she was conscious only of a yawning vacuum inside her, a vicious yearning to be held and touched and loved. She wanted to kiss him and to have him kiss her back, fiercely and possessively. She wanted him to take the fear that was haunting her and suffocate it in a consuming, life-affirming passion. Without further consideration, and without compunction, she leaned forward and pressed her lips to his.

The kiss was tentative, careful, plaintive, and Seb recognized the hunger roiling beneath the surface. When she lifted her hands to frame his face, stroking the corners of his mouth with her thumbs, he knew he could do nothing to prevent what was about to happen between them. He had brought her here to his apartment for recovery, not seduction. In fact, up until this moment, he had been too preoccupied in mulling over the accident to even consider the idea. But now, suddenly, the choice was upon him, and he knew his options had evaporated into this one inevitable conclusion. He could refuse, of course, could remind her of all the reasons this impulsive act should not occur, but already her need had permeated his reason. With the touch of her lips, he was hers.

He knew that she was experiencing a wild ride of roller-coaster emotions...emotions that had to be expressed and expunged. A devastating demand spiraled from her touch and ricocheted throughout his body, communicating in a language he couldn't misunderstand. She needed the comfort of human contact, the vitality of an act of consummation, the most fundamental affirmation that she was still alive.

He worked his hands into her hair and felt her body give, pulling him back with her against the chair cushions. One kiss dissolved into another, lush and desperate with promise. She tensed as his arms went around her, trembled as he took command of the embrace and then shifted and slid off the chair onto the floor, pulling him down with her.

Her hands ran feverishly over his back and tangled into his hair. Every fiber of his being responded to her, wanted her, cared nothing for the outcry of his conscience for self-discipline and resistance. She was more tempting than he had thought possible. Desire seared his veins with a steady flame of longing, and passion blazed white-hot and irresistible in his groin. He needed her...more than he had needed anyone or anything for a very long time. He wanted her with a desperation that alarmed and excited him. Her kisses lured him like a siren's call, implored him to forget the art of seduction, urged him to bury himself inside her and satisfy this terrible, wondrous craving.

A shuddery breath escaped her, as soft as midnight, as gentle as the moon's surrender to the sun, and as it brushed his skin with tantalizing warmth, he struggled to regain some control. She was desirable, yes, but she was vulnerable, too. She deserved an act of tender and disciplined lovemaking, not a mindless coupling of bodies. He wanted to pleasure her, wanted to hear her cries of satisfaction, wanted to know that the moments they shared were equally gratifying. Yet even as he tried to restrain his wildfire impulses, she reached for him again, her hands stroking down across his shoulders, his midriff, settling on the hard evidence that convicted him without remorse.

"Sebastian."

Her wistful whisper was a prayer and his undoing. He couldn't have resisted now if heaven had opened and the angels had commanded him to stop. She was the seed of his father's enemy. She was his destiny. Sin or salvation, he had to have her.

Moving quickly, he captured her wrists in his hands and rolled her onto her back beneath him. He straddled her hips, pinned her arms above her head and stared in helpless fascination at the alluring slant of her lips and the fearless passion in her eyes. Her luxuriant hair was a pool of fire around her head, its silken tendrils curling and teasing his fingertips.

She moved under his weight, pressing upward against his thighs, invoking his most erotic thoughts. As her chest rose and fell with the labored effort of her breathing, he lowered his head and mouthed the tip of her breast, testing her willingness through the fabric of her clothes. Her nipple pebbled in reply, pushing up against the wet fabric, preening for his tongue, begging for more and more and more of his touch.

A blinding rush of sensuality writhed inside her, and Monty closed her eyes, concentrating on the unfamiliar, bone-searing passion that possessed her. She had never experienced such uninhibited need. Perhaps this intense desire to prove she was alive was a normal, deeply human reaction to having been in danger. Perhaps it was as simple as a *coup de foudre,* a flash of lightning, the French "love at first sight." Perhaps she was falling in love with this mysterious man who kindled the fire that now burned hot and liquid in her belly.

When he released her hands and brought his palm to cup and knead her breast, the world stopped, but the timelessness of her feelings spun on and on. Nothing else existed. Not the thin, serviceable rug on which she lay. Not the distant sounds of traffic and civilization. Not the magic that was Paris. Nothing remained in her consciousness except him and the wondrous way he made her feel.

She pressed up against him, wanting to feel his lean, hard body on top of hers. Her pulse raced—faster and faster—drumming the beat of desire into her head as well as imprinting it in her heart. The shivers that coursed through her were exciting, utterly treacherous, and she had no more power over them than she had over the rain which was even now pelting the window outside.

He captured her mouth again and yet again, seizing the sweetness from her lips, commandeering them in a slow, torturous domination. His possession was thorough and complete, as if he had to prove to himself that she was real and that the invitation on her lips was genuine.

The kiss flowered and bloomed, heavily laden with rich, sensual promise. If lightning had struck her at that moment, sealing her doom, Monty knew she would have bargained with the devil, himself, to remain alive long enough to enjoy the fruition of that promise. She couldn't help believing, too, that if lightning did strike, Seb would follow her into hell and bring her back to finish the seduction she had begun.

His breathing grew labored with restraint and flowed into and over her like a hot, drenching shower. She brushed the tip of her tongue across the soft, sensuous lining of his lips and found delight in his quick response. A scalding, eager ache throbbed low inside her, and a sharp, scintillating need twisted itself into her very being.

She would never be the same after this experience. That much she knew and accepted. What she would be after this, however, was a mystery to which only Sebastian held the key. What she was at this moment was a woman in need of solace, a woman who had borrowed another's identity so she might know love in its purest form. She had bought love in her lifetime and paid for it with disillusionment and self-doubt. Now, she would discover how it felt to be wanted for herself... not for her wealth, her life-style, her power. Montgomery Carlisle. Stripped of the accoutrements of her name. Divested of her wealth. And what was left was an ordinary woman desired by a truly splendid man. The idea brought a feeling of incredible, unbelievable freedom.

His hand slipped beneath the waistband of her jeans, loosed the hem of her blouse and glided softly, but urgently, across the smooth planes of her stomach to reach her breast. He pushed beneath the elastic of her bra, releasing her sensitized flesh to fill his palm. Desire suffused her and she arched upward, bringing her nipple into aching contact with his searching fingers. A throaty moan escaped her as he lowered his head and fondled the rosy peak with his tongue.

A restless commotion swirled inside her, building into a solid, undeniable torrent of physical longing. His body was tightly muscled beneath her hands and hardened by the exertion of supporting his own weight to keep from crushing her. His arms, his chest, his thighs, the sinewy cording of his buttocks, all were taut testimonials to his self-restraint. And there was no denying the level of his arousal... the hard evidence was pressed firmly and irrefutably against her stomach.

Sebastian desired her... and that knowledge seduced her very soul. She didn't care what his reasons were. She didn't care if he felt anything other than a hearty, healthy lust for her. Right now, that was all she wanted—a consummation of emotions, a coupling without the complication of analysis. She wanted him. He wanted her. For the moment, that was enough.

He stroked his hands down her sides, molding her to his contours, pushing aside the impediment of her clothing, demonstrating the raw hunger of his need in unmistakable terms, returning to her lips to burn her again and again with his fire.

New sensations ran unrestrained, communicating a frenzy of impulses throughout her body. She wanted to touch him everywhere, kiss him everywhere, caress him until he cried out for her to stop... or go on. She wanted to exercise this feeling of power, bring his will around her finger and make him want her as he had never wanted anyone else. And in the same instant, she wanted to surrender completely to his greater strength, wanted to feel that he was the conqueror and she the territory he claimed for his own.

And then, the struggle for dominance vanished along with their clothes, pushed out of the way, torn and tossed aside in the frenzy to be together, naked skin against naked skin. Her body throbbed to be filled. The empty ache inside her swelled with her need and she was desperate to take him inside herself.

Her hands ran furiously over his shoulders, his back, his hips, urging him to end her agony with a swift and efficient thrust. With a hungry groan, Sebastian returned to her lips and then kissed a devastating path to her ear. *"Ma fleur, tu me fais craquer."*

Monty hugged the words close. *You shatter my heart.* Yes, her heart, too, was full to the point of bursting, of fragmenting into a million pieces, of shattering with the joyous ecstasy of the moment. "I..." She didn't know what answer to give, so she stroked her hand through the length of his hair and murmured his name in a husky, needy whisper. "Sebastian."

He traced the ridges of her ear with his tongue and teased her earlobe until she couldn't suppress her shivers of delight. "Let me love you in my own time," he said softly. "My body wants to rush, but my heart instructs me to linger...and it is always best to listen to the heart. Lie back, *petite fleur,* and allow me to pleasure you. I promise you will not be disappointed."

Her body fairly vibrated with unfulfilled longing, even as her lips curved in reluctant and tender acceptance. "The only way you could disappoint me now, Seb, is if you stopped touching me."

His gaze locked with hers for moments that extended to forever, and then, slowly, purposefully, he began the annihilation of any preconceived and innocent ideas she had about the art of making love. He was demanding, skilled and without inhibition. He was gentle, thorough and completely focused on her. Focused on every square inch of her, to be exact.

She was seduced . . . from the tip of every toe to the inner curve of her knees to the delicate skin between her fingers. He took possession of her senses, brought her hunger for him to the point of physical pain, then took another route to the same destination, bringing her to the edge of ecstasy and then, incredibly, taking her pleasure to an even higher plane. He kissed her ankles, her wrists, her thighs, her stomach, the hollows of her throat and at least a thousand other points of delight. He mapped out every intimate touch and took pleasure in returning again and again to the ones that obviously brought her the highest degree of satisfaction.

His whole and complete attention was concentrated on her for hours, or perhaps days—Monty was incapable of counting—and she was helpless to do more than cherish the sweet inclusiveness of his seduction. But she also was accustomed to having her own way, and she couldn't keep her hands off the intriguing slope of his back and the interesting texture of his thighs. When he groaned deep in his throat, she knew his control was worn paper thin.

She opened her arms and her body and he came into her, fully aroused and swollen with desire. His first thrust united their bodies, and with eyes closed in pleasure, he rocked inside her. Then, gently, firmly, he positioned her legs around him and began to move rhythmically in and out, in and out, until Monty thought she would dissolve with the sensations.

The rippling convulsion that shook her body possessed every part of her, heart and soul. He tensed and then leaned in to kiss her lips, passionately and possessively, as he burst inside her, carrying her with him in a dizzy plunge of absolute fulfillment.

Gradually, his kiss eased into an embrace of utter tenderness, and he relaxed against her with a soft sigh. *"Tu es belle,"* he whispered. *"Tu es belle."*

And lying in his arms, thoroughly loved, deliciously sated, Monty had never felt more beautiful.

"MADEMOISELLE CARLISLE could be worried." Sebastian's voice rumbled low in his chest, the sound muffled and hollow sounding beneath her ear. He pressed a soft kiss on the top of her head and she rubbed her bare legs across his in a lazy, feline stretch.

"I can assure you that at this moment, Mademoiselle Carlisle isn't worried about a single thing."

His chuckle was like a soothing massage. "Perhaps she isn't, but wouldn't it be a good idea to telephone the château, anyway?"

Eve. Seb believed she was Eve, not Montgomery Carlisle. Abruptly, Monty recalled the other party to her identity switch, and she realized there was a good possibility that Eve *was* worried. There was an even better possibility she'd overreact to Monty's absence, call Edwin, and then there'd be hell to pay. "I probably should let her know we won't be back tonight."

"It isn't too late, if you wish to return."

"Well, I don't wish," she said. "I want to spend the night with you. I want to wake up in your bed tomorrow morning, hearing the sounds you hear, feeling your arms around me, your lips against mine."

"Ambitious agenda." He shifted away from her and sat up. "I'll place the call to the château, and then you can put *mademoiselle's* mind at rest."

Monty was almost certain that a phone call announcing she was spending the night with Sebastian wasn't going to put Eve's mind at rest, but she nodded her agreement, anyway.

Within a matter of minutes, Eve's worried voice filled her ear. "Where are you?"

"Paris."

"Where in Paris? The Ritz? Are you staying overnight at the hotel?"

Monty smiled across the room at Sebastian, who waved his hand as he walked, naked, from the room. "I have a room with a view."

"But I thought you'd be back here by now. It's getting late." Eve's voice picked up the whine of a jealous child. "Are you staying in the city tonight?"

"Yes. The delay is ... unavoidable."

Eve's weary sigh sounded as if it had journeyed around the world and back. "So, you're all right?"

"Never better. Did you have a pleasant day?"

"It was all right. I finished a book and started another."

"And I picked up a new one for you this afternoon at Shakespeare & Company."

"You were there this afternoon?"

Monty wasn't going to cause any more concern by confiding her near miss with the dark sedan. "You asked me to pick up the book for you and I did. Of course I was there."

A moment of silence echoed across the wire. "Where's Sebastian?"

"Why? Do you want to talk to him?"

"Of course not. But I wanted to tell you. . . ." Eve's voice dropped to a remote whisper. "Louis is back. He just kind of appeared this evening. I walked into the kitchen to get my dinner tray and he was there. It was spooky. Almost like he's been here all along."

Monty felt the tug of impatience and wished Eve didn't scan every new face for possible menace. "Does he look anything like a ghost?"

"No, and he didn't fly in like a vampire, either." There was a pause as the snap was smoothed from her ruffled voice. "I suppose he must have driven in sometime this afternoon. There's a dark gray sedan parked outside that wasn't here before."

A dark gray sedan. Her mind's eye was suddenly filled with a moving picture of the car barreling toward her. Monty swallowed a sudden tightness in her throat. "Nothing unusual about that, is there?" she asked. "I mean, it's just an ordinary car.... Isn't it?"

"I guess so. Ask Sebastian. It belongs to him."

"Sebastian?" Monty made a hollow echo of the word. He looked over and smiled, oblivious to the doubt that buzzed her thoughts like a persistent mosquito. "Oh, I don't think so," Monty said, swatting aside the ridiculous idea. "He has a motorcycle, a Moto Guzzi. We've been driving all over Paris on it."

"A motorcycle?" Eve sounded horrified. "What were you thinking? You could have had an accident. Motorcycles are so very dangerous. Really, Miss Carlisle, you should be more careful. Especially considering...well, you know, the curse and all. You should take extra care, at least until your birthday."

The last Carlisle will die on the eve of her twenty-seventh birthday. Monty frowned. For the life of her, she couldn't remember if she was supposed to die on the eve of her birthday or on the actual day of her birth. Even now, after all that had happened, she couldn't take the prophecy seriously. "If I see a birthday cake with twenty-seven dangerous-looking candles on it, I promise I'll run for my life."

"I'm serious, now. Accidents can happen in the blink of an eye."

Monty knew that firsthand. She knew, too, that she couldn't spend her life being afraid, couldn't be constantly on guard, waiting for the next car to fly out of nowhere and come barreling toward her. She wasn't going to be a target any more than she was going to allow herself to be a victim.

"I'll see you tomorrow." Monty wound the conversation to a close. "Have a nice evening there in the old castle. Curl up with a scary ghost story or a good murder mystery. And don't worry about me."

"I get paid to worry."

"You're off duty tonight. I'll see you tomorrow."

Eve's sigh was long and drawn out. "So you're at the Ritz and you're staying until tomorrow. I really wish you'd reconsider, Miss Carlisle."

"Impossible, I'm in Paris, the city where second thoughts are never allowed. Now, good night and remember, worry is a waste of time and energy." Monty hung up the phone before any further protests could be lodged. She turned as Seb entered the room, conscious suddenly that she was as naked as he. "She worries too much."

He nodded as he removed the cork on a bottle of wine. "Some people do that."

"Seb?" Monty tilted her head to the side. "Do you own a car?"

"Yes." His eyebrows lifted in slight surprise before he turned away and retrieved two glasses from a cabinet. "I keep it at the château."

She wanted to ask him if it was a dark gray sedan, if it had tinted windows and a new dent in the hood. But the car that had gunned for her that afternoon couldn't be Sebastian's car. And even if it were, Sebastian had been with her.

Of course, Louis could have been driving the car. There would have been time after the accident for him to drive back. But Louis didn't know her, couldn't possibly have known where to watch for her on the street and...

Charlotte had been present when the day's errands had been mapped out. She could have told Louis the itinerary, could have mentioned Shakespeare & Company. Charlotte was Louis's wife. She could have told him where to make the hit.

Make the hit?

Monty rubbed her forehead. She must be losing her mind. What had happened today was an accident. A car going too fast and swerving to miss a second car that pulled into its path. That was a reasonable explanation, and Eve simply had her imagining danger where none existed.

"Would you like a glass of wine before I begin the next seduction?" Seb asked with a wicked smile.

The bottle of burgundy was displayed for her approval, and Monty decided danger came in many shapes and sizes. And right now, she had a serious desire to take hold of the danger named Sebastian de Vergille. She knew just where to take hold of him, too.

"I'll have some wine," she said. "One glass after each seduction."

He considered that for a moment. "That seems fair." And he poured the wine.

THE PLAN WAS NOT going well.

Montgomery Carlisle should have been dead by now. Dead and out of the picture. It would have been so easy there in the streets of Paris. A tragic accident. A hit-and-run. And instead, another near miss. A second failure.

The next accident would have to be more carefully orchestrated. The next accident would need to be plotted and executed with the utmost prudence, the greatest attention to every small detail.

Yes, attention to detail was the best strategy. That way, the next accident would be the last accident. . . . And the last hurrah for the last of the Carlisles.

Chapter Eight

The wind whipped around her helmet and raveled the ends of her hair, fluffing it like fringe on a blanket. She dipped her head a little deeper behind Seb and leaned into the curve of his back. His hair was secured at the nape and extended beneath the lower rim of his helmet, where the strands flicked her face in a haphazard caress. She liked the blend of rushing air and the subtle scent of the man in her arms. She liked the supple feel of his jacket against her palms and the sinewy leanness of his body beneath the leather. She liked the broad muscled slope of his shoulders and the disciplined symmetry of his back. She liked everything about Sebastian...liked him more than she thought it prudent to acknowledge. They were on the Moto Guzzi, halfway to the château, and she couldn't shake the feeling that she had made a mistake by spending the night with Seb.

Not that she hadn't enjoyed the experience. It had been wonderful—beyond wonderful. But Seb had been distant all morning. He hadn't been in bed when she awakened.... She'd found him in the other room, staring at the rooftops of Paris through the flat's tall windows as he nursed a cup of coffee. And when she slipped up behind him and put her arms around him, he had stiffened. He'd recovered quickly and pulled her into his embrace, but she hadn't anticipated that first less-than-gratifying reaction. His kiss, too, had seemed perfunctory and forced. Nothing like the kisses he'd delivered the night before. And instead of directing her body back into his bed, he'd directed her attention to the view from the window.

To be fair, Paris was an incredible city, full of life and energy and undiluted romance. Seeing it awaken from the window of Seb's apartment, while she stood in his embrace, could have been an uplifting and intimate experience. But he had been distracted, distant, and Monty had a sick feeling that he regretted having spent the night with her.

"Look. There." Sebastian's voice in her ear startled her and Monty lifted her head, turning in the direction he pointed. Vineyards, green and copious, stretched through sloping fields that bordered the roadway as far as she could see. In the distance, she could just make out a line of rooftops.... The buildings of a small farm, perhaps. Or one of the villages that still existed along the Loire. A shadow crossed the field of grapevines, and Monty glanced upward to find the source...a brightly colored hot-air balloon that drifted overhead like a paper boat on a slow-moving sea.

"I wish we were up there," she said into the mouthpiece of her helmet. She felt, rather than saw, his nod of understanding. The sight was breathtaking, and she watched the balloon scale the blue sky until the motorcycle cruised too far and too fast down the roadway, and the peaceful picture shrank progressively to the size of a mural, a photograph, a postcard, a stamp, and then disappeared entirely into the distance.

Distance. Which brought her thoughts right back to Sebastian and the same inevitable conclusion. If she was having second thoughts—and she was—then why did it bother her to think that Seb might be having them, too?

It bothered her because she'd deceived him, however worthy or unworthy her reasoning, and now she had to wonder how he was going to feel when he discovered he'd slept with Montgomery Carlisle. He was bound to find out. She had never intended for the masquerade to become a fraud, just a simple way of keeping herself entertained during what she'd envisioned as a dull and boring exile. The plan had never been foolproof, and now Monty was beginning to feel like the biggest fool of all.

She could imagine that he would be quite angry with her when he found out about the deception. On the other hand, if he'd known who she was from the beginning, there wouldn't have been a night with Seb.... And she would brave anything, even his rejection, for the sake of the hours already spent in his arms.

There wasn't an easy resolution to this unexpected dilemma, she realized. She could hardly tap him on the shoulder and announce her true identity through her now dented helmet transmitter. That would be incredibly tacky, not to mention risky. He might wreck the Moto Guzzi and she'd have to offer to buy him another one and... Well, it just didn't bear thinking about.

Still, the deception ate away at her, chipping the edges of the memories she'd made the previous night, marring a delicate and beautiful happening with the hateful "what ifs" of tomorrow. She tightened her arms about his waist and held on, hoping the fantasy wouldn't fade into an unpleasant reality too soon.

Her arms squeezed into his sides, and Seb felt her nearness squeeze his heart with a new awareness. He should never have taken her to his apartment. He should have insisted they return to the château yesterday. But it was too late for regrets. They were lovers, now.

Montgomery Carlisle was his lover.

The very thought filled him with both annoyance and a breathtaking awe. She was his. She, the present owner of the de Vergilles' rightful estate. She, the great-granddaughter of the man who had destroyed his family and stolen his heritage. She, the woman who had shattered his heart with her passion.

For his own purpose, he had enlisted her help in his search of the château. He had deceived her by omitting to tell her the truth. He had tried to use her masquerade to his own advantage, plied her with subtle questions, tried to discover what she knew about the disappearing furnishings of the château. He had told her he had no interest in reclaiming the château, when if given the chance, he'd overturn her claim in an instant. If the chalice were real, if it contained the treasure that family legend declared, he wouldn't hesitate to challenge her possession of the Château de Vergille.

As the owner of the château, she was an obstacle to his search and to his future. As his lover, she represented a pure and basic jeopardy to him. He knew that as well. He had seen her in moonlight... and was bewitched. He understood that she would not forgive him when she realized he had known all along who she was. She would forever believe his lovemaking had a motive other than desire, and she would shatter his heart with her hatred.

She was out of his reach and always would be. She was a princess and he was her gardener—a mere pauper, compared to her. There was no point even in hoping for a future with her. But she was a risk he couldn't avoid. A challenge from which he couldn't back down. A fire that would undoubtedly burn his best intentions and leave his heart a scorched wasteland.

He didn't see how any good could come of this. And yet he could not desert her now. She was in danger. Mortal danger. And no matter how tarnished his armor, he was the only knight available to save her.

"I WAS AFRAID SOMETHING had happened to you."
Eve's admonishing words were the first to greet Monty
as she swung her leg across the motorcycle seat and
stepped onto the graveled drive. "I couldn't sleep a
wink last night for worrying about you."

"*Bonjour* to you, too." Monty accepted the sacks
Seb took from the storage unit of the motorcycle. She,
in turn, handed the sacks to Eve. "Greetings, *made-moiselle,* from the City of Lights. Here are the items
you requested. No thanks are necessary. Sebastian and
I are happy to have been of service." Her tone of voice
produced the desired effect. Eve's mouth closed in a
tight line, but she said nothing else to indicate her disapproval.

Charlotte was impervious to tone of voice, however, and once everyone had gathered in the spacious
but surprisingly cozy kitchen, she proceeded to fuss.
"I don't know how many times I've told you to get rid
of that stupid motorcycle, Sebastian. It's not a fit ve-
hicle for man nor beast. And to think you took Miss
O'Halloran riding on it with you. Some days I think
you don't have a lick of sense."

Seb winked across the table at Monty, and she felt
the conspiratorial bond of two children being scolded
for playing outdoors without buttoning their coats.

Charlotte shook her fuzzy head and rattled on as
she rattled pots and pans. "And you got soaked to the
bone, yesterday, didn't you? All that rain. I told Louis
last night that you'd come back with a deathly chill.
And I was right, wasn't I? One or both of you are

probably going to start sneezin' and hackin' at any minute.''

Seb's eyebrows lifted with interest. "Louis is back?''

"He's back,'' she informed Seb, as she set two mugs of steaming *chocolat chaud* on the table. "Got in late yesterday evening and tried to get the generator up and running. Probably could have done it, too, if you'd been here to help.''

"Where is he?'' Seb asked.

"You mean, now?'' Charlotte scooted a mug in front of him and one in front of Monty, then wiped her beefy hands on the corner of her apron. "I sent him to the *boulangerie* in the village to get the ba-guettes for dinner. But he's probably propping up a table at the café, and we won't see him before bed-time. You know Louis isn't one to hurry home.''

"And why should he?'' Seb teased lightly. "You'll just fuss over him.''

"He needs fussin' over. Just like you do.'' Her pale, rheumy gaze switched to Monty. "And just like you. Now, drink that chocolate while it's hot enough to do your body some good.''

"Thank you, but I'm not thirsty.'' Monty pushed the mug aside.

Charlotte pushed it back. "You won't be thirsty if you die of pneumonia, neither. Now, drink that be-fore you come down sick.''

Sebastian murmured in French, something that Monty roughly translated to mean, "Mind your own business, you bossy old chicken." Monty bent her head, letting the waves of her chestnut hair swing forward to hide her understanding as well as her smile.

Charlotte didn't even bother to look offended. She simply shrugged and eyed the cup of hot chocolate in front of Monty with clear meaning.

Obediently, Monty picked up the mug and took a sip of the rich beverage. She felt very "mothered" all of a sudden, and the feeling was unusual, but not unpleasant. Her own mother had died so long ago she wasn't even a memory, and even had she lived, Monty didn't think she would have been terribly maternal. Aunt Josephine wasn't motherly, either. She was a worrywart, and the concern she showed Monty was all mixed up with her grab bag of myths and stories, which wasn't anything like Charlotte's mother-hen type of concern. After receiving just one uncompromising look from under Charlotte's spiked, sparse eyebrows, Monty was willing to drink her hot chocolate down to the very last drop and lick her lips afterward.

Obviously satisfied, Charlotte swung her attention back to Seb, making sure he, too, was taking her wonder cure. "Now, drink up," she said. "It'll be a miracle if you're not already running a fever."

Seb obediently took a drink. "Was Louis's business in Paris...successful?"

Charlotte glanced at Monty before lifting her shoulder in a rounded shrug. "What do I know? Louis never has much to say."

"And you like him that way."

"Maybe I do," Charlotte said, "and maybe I don't. But I would like to have some electricity."

"Electricity would be nice." Monty seconded the opinion.

"Don't you enjoy candlelight?"

Seb's question was softly teasing, and Monty thought she might drown in the ardent darkness of his eyes. Electricity, she decided, was overrated. "It would be nice to have the option of using a hair dryer, if I wanted."

Having declined a cup of *chocolat chaud,* Eve had been fidgeting with the book Monty had bought for her at Shakespeare & Company. She looked up with a frown. "Well, I'm sick and tired of stumbling around in the dark, and I think I'll just call Edwin and get something done about . . . well, about everything that isn't being done around here." Having said her piece, she resumed flipping pages and made it fairly obvious that she had no more regard for the castle's caretakers than she had for the quaint custom of warding off a chill with a cup of hot chocolate.

"That's a good idea, Miss Carlisle. Why don't you do that? Phone Edwin and get something done." Monty couldn't restrain the irritation that shadowed the suggestion. Personally, she found the kitchen warm, the unfamiliar fussing comforting and the chocolate a pleasant touch.

As silly as it seemed, Eve was behaving as if she were jealous. Seb was undeniably attractive, and perhaps

Eve's heart, too, beat a little faster when he was in the room. Maybe Eve was jealous of the attention Monty was receiving. Then again, it might not be jealousy at all, but a simple impatience with an experience Eve found unremarkable. While Monty delighted in the perfect ordinariness of sitting in a kitchen, drinking a mug of hot chocolate and listening to Charlotte's roughshod gentleness, Eve obviously didn't appreciate the novelty.

Her loss, Monty thought, as a pleasant degree of lethargy invaded her body. She liked the idea that Seb was seated across from her, drinking chocolate from an identical mug, being fussed over and cared about. There were definite advantages to being "just one of the employees."

Suddenly, a sound, a deep and distant boom, reverberated through the château. Charlotte planted her palms on the tabletop and looked around. "That sounded kind of like a gunshot."

"It sounded *exactly* like a gunshot." Seb slammed his mug down onto the table, pitching loops of milky chocolate across the surface as he shoved back his chair.

Monty thrust back her own chair and rose to follow him, but Eve grabbed her arm and detained her. "That was a g-g-gunshot?"

"I don't know, but I'm certainly going to find out." Monty shook off the detaining arm and hurried after Seb as he raced across the kitchen and up the stairs.

As she ran after him, Monty thought irrelevantly about the confusing design of the château. Stairways started on one floor and swept upward in a narrow ribbon to end abruptly at the floor above, only to begin again at the opposite end of the floor landing and rise upward to the next floor. Seb had explained that the inconvenient arrangement had been built into the architecture as a line of defense. If the castle walls had ever been breached, the stairways would create the maximum degree of confusion and difficulty in gaining entrance to the next section of the castle. The château residents would have had time to escape, or at least have had the advantage in a fight on their home turf. It had probably been an ingenious means of outwitting the enemy at one time, but now that the age of attacking and conquering kingdoms had passed, it seemed merely like a way to force the residents to exercise.

And this was exercise, she thought, as she reached the top of the stairs and stepped into the great hall. Charlotte lumbered up the stairs behind her, huffing and puffing as she tried to keep pace. At the far side of the cavernous hall, Seb was disappearing into the library.

"Where is he going?" Monty asked.

"The...wine cellars," Charlotte gasped out. "There's a...a passageway...in there...in the library."

"A secret passageway?"

"Not...anymore."

Monty ran to the library and had barely paused in the archway before she saw the displaced wall panel and the dark opening behind it. Unhesitating, she hurried forward, slipped behind the panel and started down a dark and dingy stairwell. Behind her, she could hear Charlotte fussing under her ragged breath about castles and generators and narrow stairs. Farther back, Eve was all chattering teeth and nervous protests.

"Don't go down there. Stay up here. Wait! Don't leave me alone up here." And down the stairs she, too, came.

Over the muffled protests of the other women, Monty could hear Seb's hurried footsteps ahead of her. "Seb?" she called. "Where are you?"

"There." Charlotte's voice came over Monty's left shoulder, and her stubby finger pointed out a door silhouetted by a light on the other side. "That's the garage."

"I thought you said this led to the wine cellar."

"This part's a garage. The rest is wine cellar.... Or at least it once was."

"Why didn't someone bring a lantern?" Eve demanded from two steps up.

Monty braced herself with a hand against the wall and moved toward the partially opened door and the rays of light that streaked the darkness around it.

"Seb?" She touched the door, swinging it back with the barely audible sigh of a well-oiled hinge. She stepped through the doorway, blinking against the sunlight that streamed through an open pair of wooden doors on the opposite side of a gray weathered-looking barn of a room. Beyond the open door, a nubby strip of concrete fashioned a slanting driveway. Dust particles coated the air like a thick fog settling slowly into place. The vague, musty odor that resided in many parts of the château blended with the dust and a milky, acidic smell. There was a slight metallic, powdery scent fading quickly in the outside air.

"Seb?" Monty called.

"Over here." A car, partially covered with a dingy tarp, was parked between her and the sound of his voice, and she moved around it to reach his side. He was crouched beside another door, which was partially open, and at his feet lay a man who, except for his dark gray wool slacks and drab gray plaid vest, looked for all the world like Santa Claus. Fluffy white beard, round belly, snowy white head of hair and all. At the moment, the spots of color in his cheek and on the tip of his nose stood out like red apples against the pallor of his face. And in the center of his broad forehead was a puffy, angry-looking goose egg of a bruise.

"Louis." Charlotte moved past Monty and knelt across from Seb, panic crinkling her eyes into worried slits. "Is he all right?"

"He seems to be coming around," Seb said. "Hold him still while I take a closer look."

He was looking for blood, Monty realized, and any indication of a gunshot wound. Holding her breath, she leaned back against the car and waited. Of course he'd be all right. He had to be. No one could shoot Santa. Not in her garage.

Eve hesitated on the other side of the car. "Is he dead? Did someone shoot him?"

Seb's hands moved over the inert body, pushing, probing and finally lifting the white head onto his lap. At the movement, Louis let out a low and heartfelt groan. The network of lines around his eyes wrinkled with pain, and he lifted a chubby hand to rub the side of his head. A few low and somber French phrases tumbled from his lips, but Monty chose not to translate. She concentrated, instead, on looking for signs of a struggle, clues as to who else had been in the garage and why. So intent was her search for clues, that it took several seconds to register the most obvious one—a long, double-barreled shotgun laying on the packed dirt floor at her feet.

"There it is," she said in a half whisper. "The gun."

Sebastian barely glanced her way. He shifted position and gently examined the lump on Louis's forehead. "What were you shooting at, Louis?"

"Shooting?" Monty echoed in surprise. "*Louis* did the shooting?"

Seb gave her a slight frown before returning his attention to the older man. "Can you remember why you came down to the garage?"

Louis blinked a couple of times, and Monty wasn't surprised to find that when he opened them his eyes were a perfect Santa Claus blue. "I don't remember, exactly. I must have heard a noise or something." His words collided with another low moan. "Someone hit me on the head, I guess. Is there blood anywhere?"

"You're not bleeding, you old coot." Charlotte said the words with obvious affection. She shifted her weight and took over Seb's position, intent on performing her own examination of her husband's injuries. "Your head's too hard to have any blood in it, anyway."

He shook his head impatiently. "No, no. I thought I might have hit whoever was in here."

"I thought you didn't do any shooting," Seb reminded him.

"I didn't remember," he snapped. "Now, I do. I came in from outside and—ow! Woman, don't go touching that bump on my head again, do you hear?"

Charlotte nodded and went right on measuring the bump with her fingertips. Monty pressed the heels of her hands against the rough tarp and watched Seb as he straightened and began a slow inspection of the area. Monty pushed away from the car to follow him. The nearby door was unlatched and swayed in and out, like a gate half-off its hinges and vulnerable to the wind. "Where does this lead?" she asked.

"To the wine cellars, from which there are a number of exits. Whoever was here could be on the other side of the château or halfway to the village by now." Seb supplied the answer with a frown. "This entrance is usually kept locked. No one uses the garage here anymore."

Monty glanced at the car. "So what's that? A ghostmobile?"

"That's my BMW," Seb answered distractedly. "I stored it here until Louis and I have time to do a few repairs on it."

Louis winced as he moved to get up, and Charlotte helped him to his feet. "I heard a noise as I was coming back from town. The outside doors were open and I thought that was strange." He touched the knot on his head, then stroked the marshmallow puff that was his beard. "So I got my gun."

Seb reached up high on the stone wall and touched a hole the size of a turkey platter. "And you tried to turn this rock wall into a crater."

Louis was obviously not in a jolly humor. "I tried to catch whoever was in here, but when I sneaked up to this door, somebody gave it a hard push. It flew back and hit me square on the head. I don't remember anything after that."

"The gun fired as you fell," Seb concluded.

"It's a wonder you didn't shoot your eye out." Charlotte smoothed Louis's jacket, flicking off the dust and debris. "Let's go upstairs and take care of that bump."

Monty was relieved that the explanation was relatively simple. "It's lucky the gun wasn't pointing at the car when it went off."

Eve had been hovering like a timid mouse, but as Charlotte led Louis past her she found her voice. "It looks like something happened to it. There's a scratch or something...." She leaned over the partially exposed hood of the BMW.

"What?" Louis reached for the tarp cover and jerked it back and off, revealing a dark gray sedan.

"It's been damaged." Eve traced a fingertip across a small dent in the metal. When she lifted her finger, a dark streak marred the peachy tint of her skin and she rubbed at the stain. "The paint's coming off."

Monty fought a tingling sensation in her stomach and a dizziness that buzzed in her ears. Like a marionette, she moved forward to touch the dent, to feel the grit of the rubbing compound, to see the mark on her finger and know that someone had, just recently, tried to remove the black streaks from the hood of the car.

Her memory flashed back to yesterday, to the bookstore, to the rainy Paris street—to the dark sedan that had been aiming for her. She could see the car, dark gray with tinted windows. She could see the motorcycle helmet fly out of her hands into the air and then come down, with a thick smacking sound, on the hood. The helmet had bounced on, smashing into the windshield of the other car, and the dark sedan had roared away into the storm. But the helmet had left a mark. She knew that now. A shallow dent and a pucker of black streaks. Just like the marks that any fool could clearly see on the hood of Sebastian's dark gray sedan.

Chapter Nine

"It's the Carlisle curse." Eve's hushed whisper bobbed like a helium balloon in the heavy silence of Monty's bedchamber. "If everything you've just told me is true, then there isn't a moment to waste. We should get away from the château as quickly as possible."

Monty stopped contemplating the Joan of Arc tapestry and turned her head to look at Eve, who was sitting cross-legged on the end of the bed. She thought the scene would make a nice snapshot in a travel guide—two young women sitting on a canopied bed in a château in France. *Friends sharing secrets at Château Carlisle,* the caption might read. She sent the image packing and focused on Eve's melodramatics. "I came to the château to get away from the curse, remember?"

"But the accidents. A massive statue nearly falls on you, then you trip and fall on a secret stairway and then you're almost flattened by a speeding car—a car which then turns up in the garage downstairs. It's as if the curse is actually going to come true." Eve shivered and hugged her arms. "I wish you'd consider leaving."

"I have considered it." Monty rested her head on her upraised knees. "But it makes no sense to turn tail and run without attempting to find out why the accidents happened."

"You could get yourself killed, snooping around."

Monty lifted her head and settled a pensive look on her companion. "I don't think so, Eve. I've never believed there was any truth to that ridiculous Carlisle curse, and I wish you'd forget you ever heard about it. The accidents were just that...accidents. Nothing more than coincidences. You're imagining evil where none exists."

"I didn't imagine the marks on that car downstairs." Eve paused and then added slyly, "Sebastian's car."

Courage punctured by the reminder, Monty closed her eyes and tried to erase the memory of those marks, the sick feeling that had scoured her with suspicion, left her confused and not knowing who or what to believe. "He wasn't driving it in Paris," she stated flatly. "We took the Moto Guzzi."

"You didn't see who was driving the car," Eve pointed out. "And even if he wasn't behind the wheel, who else knew where you'd be and when?"

Conspiracy, Monty interpreted from the comment, and knew she didn't like that theory any better. "It was a coincidence," she insisted, more for her own benefit than for Eve's reassurance. "An accident that could have happened, but didn't. I wasn't hurt, you know."

"You're naive to believe this isn't directed at you, Monty. How could it be a coincidence that the car that nearly ran you down in Paris is parked in the garage at your château?"

The questions buzzed her like a dive-bomber, and she wished she could shut them out by covering her ears. "I don't know, Eve. I can't explain any of this, but I won't believe Sebastian is involved. He just isn't."

Eve rocked back, never letting up on the intense, accusing gaze she kept fastened on Monty. "You're thinking with your heart, not your head. He's so involved, he's practically advertising it, and you're acting like a complete fool."

With a lift of her eyebrows, Monty requested Eve's apology. None was forthcoming. Eve held her ground with stubborn silence. "You're wrong," Monty said in a voice that was rock solid with conviction.

"Maybe," Eve replied evenly. "But if I'm not, you could turn out to be *dead* wrong, couldn't you?"

Monty grappled with the bedlam of voices inside her head. "Seb has been very concerned," she offered in defense of him and of her own judgment. "Solicitous and protective, too."

Eve's lips curled in an unpleasant little smile. "Do you think no one can fool you? That just because you're Montgomery Carlisle, because you've been pampered and cared for your entire life, no one could want to harm you?"

The words were harsh, the truth unpalatable. Monty knew loneliness up close and personal, but she suddenly felt desperately and depressingly alone. With unresolved energy, she squared her shoulders against the persistent pressure of Eve's paranoia. "I don't believe he's involved," she said in a calm voice, of which she felt unreasonably proud. "I believe Sebastian was being perfectly honest—and honorable—when he said he had no idea who could have driven his car from the château to Paris. I believe he will do everything in his power to discover who did so.... And why."

Eve sighed with deep frustration. "You also believe he just *happened* to be nearby each and every time an accident occurred. Go on believing. But don't expect me, or anyone else who cares about your safety, to look kindly on your... *lover.*"

She made the word slither, made it sound ugly and frightening. Monty tried not to be angry. Eve thought evil lurked in every corner; she was governed by fear. And she thought she was doing the job she'd been hired to do. Or else she simply feared being held responsible if anything did happen.

"You're free to leave, if you want," Monty said. "I'll see that you get your full salary and any bonus Edwin might have promised you. Please don't feel you have to stay to take care of me."

A flicker of uncertainty flared in Eve's blue eyes. "I can't leave now," she said after a few tense moments.

"I'd like to, but it just wouldn't be right." She swung her feet over the side of the mattress and slid to a standing position beside the bed. "Just so you know, I tried earlier to phone Edwin, but he was away from his office. I did talk to Aunt Josephine, however, and confided my concern to her." Eve hesitated, then continued. "The curse is real, Monty—I'm convinced of it. You'd do well to heed all the warnings you've been given. And you should be very careful who you choose to trust."

Eve walked to the door, and Monty watched her leave with mixed emotions. She was angry with her secretary for being so negative, for pointing out the inconsistencies and the evidence in each of the "accidents," and for calling Sebastian's every gesture, every word into question.

Monty had wanted to shout down the not so subtle accusation by saying that Sebastian had no motive for wanting to harm her. He thought she was Eve O'Halloran. Everyone here thought she was Eve. How could anyone at the château have known about the identity switch? Edwin had stopped allowing Monty's photograph to be published, once she'd reached adolescence, stating that it was a matter of her security. Before now, she hadn't made so much as an overnight stop at the château. She hadn't even been in France for a couple of years and Edwin had gone to a great deal of trouble to keep her destination on this trip a secret.

All of which meant nothing.

She either chose to trust or not to trust.

"What would you do, Joan?" she asked the legendary figure in the tapestry. "Follow Eve's advice and run for your life? Or put your faith in Sebastian, regardless of the evidence against him?"

Joan's expression of determination didn't waver, and she continued to hold up the banner of battle, the flag of freedom, the call for courage.

Monty took that as an encouraging sign. After all, if she was going to believe there was an ounce of truth to the Carlisle curse, then there was no reason she shouldn't believe in fairy tales, as well.

CENTURIES BEFORE, a village had grown up around the base of the château, and although the years had wrought significant changes, the essence of the past remained. Some of the village shops were still housed in buildings that had seen hundreds of yesterdays, while others had been built on top of the old foundations. The remnants of a checkered history were clearly visible in the form of a crumbling archway or a vestigial carving near the site of the present-day church—which was no youngster itself, having originated sometime in the eighteenth century.

Near the river, tall poplars shaded cottages with slate roofs and lovingly tended gardens full of roses and cabbages. The slow-moving currents of the river made a silver-streaked tapestry from the watery images of the clouds and trees reflected in its depths. The tiny town square was a respite within an oasis of time, peaceful, clean and agelessly serene. The villagers who strolled the streets went about their business with a basic savoir faire, paying little, if any, heed to the few tourists who had wandered into their midst.

Monty took in the whole scene with dispassionate eyes, from a weathered wooden bench near the square. A few steps away, the aromas wafting from the *boulangerie* were as good as anything she had ever smelled. The air was laden with fresh-baked fragrance, and the crusty croissant she'd bought should have tasted like a miracle in her mouth. Unfortunately, she was too preoccupied to appreciate the buttery flavor and flaky texture of the bread. Her thoughts were still at the château, still turning over the events of the past few days, still trying to make sense of the "accidents".... And still trying to convince her heart that she wasn't, couldn't possibly be, in love with Sebastian de Vergille.

As if her contemplation had summoned him, she saw him halfway down the street, walking toward her with a purposeful, confident stride. He was wearing dark slacks that hugged his hips in a sexy embrace, and his cream-colored shirt was discreetly buttoned almost to the neck, which somehow seemed oddly suggestive. His hair hung loose and long, unconventional and dangerously attractive. The uncompromising set of his chin called to her like a half-remembered promise.

And her silly heart renewed its argument.

But just as the smile inside her completed the journey to her lips, Sebastian stopped and looked back the way he had come. Hadn't he seen her? she wondered. She could see him so clearly, or was it just that every detail of his face was etched into her memory and was always visible in her mind's eye? He turned again, and just as she started to lift her hand in greeting, she saw his smile.... A smile of unutterable mystique and dangerous charm. Her heart stopped beating for all of a moment and then raced like an excited puppy, all eagerness and buoyant spirit.

Then someone walked up to Sebastian, coming between him and her point of view. Monty tipped her head to one side, trying to see around... It was Eve, she realized with a start. Eve, who had sashayed into Monty's fantasy. Eve, who was placing her hand on Seb's muscled forearm. Eve, who was the unlikely recipient of Sebastian's attentive and devastating smile.

Monty held her breath. Eve? she thought. What was Eve doing here with...? And then she saw Seb raise Eve's hand to his lips, saw the sensual gaze he kept fastened on Eve's face, saw the lift of Eve's shoulders as she drew a deep breath, saw Eve's expression soften with the look of a woman charmed to the tips of her toes.

Suspended between stunned disbelief and a myriad of questions, Monty watched as Sebastian kept hold of Eve's fingers with one hand as he slipped his other hand around her waist. His head bent to hers in an intimate, confiding sort of way, and the two of them walked into the village's only café, leaving Monty with a half-eaten croissant and a thickening lump of betrayal in the pit of her stomach.

An assignation. Sebastian and Eve. It was unthinkable and ironic. Eve and Sebastian. Why would he be meeting her? And why would a fearful Eve take the risk of being alone with a man she thought was untrustworthy and even dangerous?

The answer was as clear as the sound of the bell in the church tower, ringing the hour with a clarity that echoed in the quiet air. Eve had argued against Sebastian not because she feared for Monty, but because of the attraction she herself felt for him. She was unsophisticated and shy, and Seb was a man of unlimited appeal. Why wouldn't she do everything in her power to divert Monty's attention and steal him for her own?

Reluctantly, Monty forced herself to spread the blame. Sebastian couldn't be excluded from her consideration. He had deceived her—admittedly with her able assistance—and now she had to look at what had happened between them from a new and unsavory angle. Obviously, he was playing her against Eve—one against the other. Obviously, too, he had ulterior motives for these two separate romances. And it was now painfully obvious that she had been a frivolous fool.

It was easy to believe that Seb had used her to find out how to get to Montgomery Carlisle, never realizing that he was dealing with Montgomery, herself. She had pretended to be Eve in order to be ordinary, in order to be appreciated and wanted for herself. And

Sebastian had fallen in with her plans with the alacrity of an acorn falling from a tree. He had made her feel desirable and secure, safe and loved. And she had trusted him beyond reason and without hesitation.

She'd like to think the joke was on him. He was, at this very moment, working his romantic magic on the woman he believed was an American heiress, the one person who stood between him and the lost heritage of his family, the owner of the château that he felt rightfully belonged to him. Oh, yes, he'd feel pretty stupid when he discovered the identity switch, that was for sure.

But try as she might, Monty couldn't find a glimmer of humor in the thought, and she knew in her heart that the joke was on her.

WHEN SHE HEARD the faint click, Monty knew Sebastian was about to enter her bedroom. She couldn't see too well in the night-shaded dark, but she watched the wall and was able to make out the change in shadows as the hidden door moved inward. It seemed like an eternity before he appeared at the foot of her bed, and, much to her chagrin she recognized the ache of desire he instantly and effortlessly aroused in her body.

"You're awake," he said softly, as if pleased by the fact. "Ready to search for the 'Holy Grail'?"

Careful to keep her expression neutral and her traitorous longing hidden, she looked at him with a questioning lift of her eyebrow. "I don't think so. Not tonight."

His eyes took on a wary gleam in the tinted darkness. "Are you all right?"

"Fine." She sounded anything but fine, and she could see that he recognized it.

"You are upset." He moved to the side of the bed and reached for her hand, but she slipped it beneath the covers and safely away from his touch.

"Why would I be upset?" she asked in a voice that challenged him to answer.

The muscles in his jaw clinched, and his dark eyebrows drew together in a forbidding frown. "Do you want to tell me what I have done to make you angry?"

She wanted to tell him. Oh, yes indeed, she would enjoy letting him have it with both barrels, but jealousy was beneath her. He was, after all, only her gardener. "I am not angry," she lied.

His stormy gaze nearly shook her cocky "woman-wronged" attitude. And when he leaned in, keeping his eyes locked on hers, she had to fight the revealing tremor that threatened to rattle her composure from head to foot. He kissed her then, taking her lips tenderly, softly with his, asking for the answers she was refusing to give.

But she held her ground.... Somehow. Managed not to crumble beneath the onslaught of sensations his touch evoked. She might have imagined that she was madly in love with him, but he would not have the satisfaction of knowing it.

He pulled back and looked into her eyes again before he slowly released her and courteously stepped away from the bed. His chin dipped to his chest, his heels came together and he executed his trademark bow. "Very well, *mademoiselle*. I will bid you goodnight."

She had wanted an argument, wanted him to deny the irrefutable accusations she longed to fling in his face. But he was walking away, leaving the room in the same stealthy manner in which he'd entered. And she had too much pride to call him back.

But not too much to stop her from following him. By the time the hidden door slid closed, she was out of bed and looking around for her shoes. She thought about changing clothes—her thin white nightshirt was really not appropriate for the occasion—but time was of the essence. Sebastian knew the tunnels. She didn't. If she wasted so much as another minute, she might never be able to find and follow him through the passageways.

Grabbing the flashlight from the table beside the bed, she wished briefly that she could remember where she'd kicked off her shoes, and then she ran barefoot to the wall. Her search for the concealed latch that would let her enter the passageway was surprisingly brief, and just a few minutes after Sebastian had left, she was in the tunnel and moving like a wraith through the darkness.

It wasn't until she reached the archway that led to the north tower that she remembered the spiders. Up to that point, she'd kept the flashlight beam trained on her toes and the path directly in front of her. Now, suddenly, she felt the need to play the beam across the floor on either side, up the walls and over the ceiling above. The idea that she was being watched by fuzzy, long-legged creatures with little red eyes made her mouth go dry, and she moved forward a careful inch at a time.

A noise echoed faintly in the tunnel ahead of her and she stopped cold, not sure what she'd heard or exactly what she ought to do next. The flashlight beam flickered, held steady for several seconds, then flickered again. Great, she thought. Of all the things she'd left behind in the bedroom—shoes, dark clothing, insect repellent, her good sense—an extra set of Duracells would turn out to be her waterloo.

She felt ridiculous, standing in her nightshirt and bare feet inside the dark labyrinth of the château, using a frail and erratic light to search for bugs. Why had she been so stupidly impulsive? What had she hoped to discover by following Sebastian ... if, indeed, she could find him without being discovered. And just what was she going to do now? Wait for Edouard's ghost to come along and show her the way?

Ha. She was a Carlisle. If Edouard's ghost passed her way, he'd likely lead her to the south tower and push her out the window. But she couldn't go back. Her stubbornness wouldn't let her retreat. Joan of Arc wouldn't have let the thought of a few hairy-legged spiders deter her.

The sound came again, fainter this time, and Monty listened carefully, determining its location to be directly ahead of her. Sebastian would be approaching the stairs where Monty had fallen. What was he really searching for? she wondered. How valuable was the "Holy Grail" he sought? And why had he taken the trouble to enlist her help in finding it?

Curiosity mingled with resolve to shore up her courage, and Monty rapped the flashlight against her palm, renewing a steady ray of light. All right, so she'd been impulsive. But she had come this far already, the batteries were still good, and she was pressing onward. At least Joan would be proud of her.

She took one confident step and then another, stopping abruptly as a cool rush or air swept like a whirlwind around her, then vanished as if it had never been.

The Carlisle curse is real. The last heir of Josiah Carlisle will die.... Will die... Will die...

The blast of air might have been Edouard's ghost bringing a warning, but the words that were repeated over and over again inside Monty's head were clearly recognizable. Eve's voice, then Aunt Jo's and then Eve's voice again echoed the omen, dappling Monty's arms in gooseflesh, pointing at possibilities she did not want to consider.

Up until now, she had believed she wasn't afraid of anything.... With the slight exception of red-eyed spiders. But suddenly she recognized what a lie that was. She had always been afraid of the loneliness that haunted her. The specter of her great wealth was both indulgent and fearful, and it worried her. Would she live her entire life never certain if she was loved for who she was or for what she owned? Would she die not knowing whether her worth as a person was appreciated? And what if she wasn't worthy of a genuine and enduring love?

Up until she had seen him with Eve in the village, she had had no fear of Sebastian de Vergille. Even at his mysterious best, he had made her feel protected, cared for, intimately desirable, but not afraid. And that was why she had to go on, had to follow Sebastian, had to at least try to discover why her heart had led her so badly astray. She wanted to know if he was a consummate actor, who could make passionate love to her even as he was planning her death. She wanted to know what his motives were and how they were connected to whatever secret treasures lay buried inside this moldy old castle. She wanted to hear him admit he had lied.... With his kiss, with his touch, with his eyes. But most of all, she wanted to hear him say the words that would break her heart but set her free.

Bravely, she stepped forward, careful only of the uncertain flooring beneath her bare feet. Stopping only to listen for the muffled sounds of his footsteps ahead, she made her way to the stairs and cautiously used the railing to guide her as she descended to the floor below.

The passageway widened here, and she could more easily make out the doorways that opened off it. She almost stumbled over the fallen statue and could see the marks on the floor where Charlotte had scooted the angel into its present position inside the tunnel. Farther on, another pathway branched off from the first and she decided to follow it. The sound of footsteps had long since faded, and there were too many turns and twists to allow for any sighting of a light moving in the darkness ahead. One direction now seemed to offer as good a possibility of finding Sebastian as any other.

Her first step in that direction brought her foot into contact with a sharp bit of rock, and she jumped back with a soft cry of pain. The sound died instantly as she felt the hard wall of a human chest against her back and the unyielding grip of two very strong arms around her waist. The flashlight fell from her hand and connected with the floor in a metallic clunk. The light went out. Her heart jumped to her throat, and her breath squeezed out in a painful wheeze.

"Why are you following me?" Seb's voice rasped in her ear and his hold on her tightened. "And where the hell did you leave your shoes?"

Monty had two conflicting reactions. First, that he had chosen a perfect place for a murder. And second, that if he meant to kill her, he surely wouldn't have noticed her bare feet. She swallowed hard. "I was looking for—for you."

"For what reason?"

"I, uh, changed my mind."

"Regarding what?"

"About... Tonight. I decided to—to come with you."

"Why?"

She wished he would ask her an easy question. "Well, because..."

He waited, his breath stirring the hair at her temple with short, uneven puffs. His body was a blanket of heat, warming her against the cold, of which she was suddenly, chillingly, aware. His arms offered a protective intimacy, and she closed her eyes to shut out the grim reality that his every action was a lie.

But even as she acknowledged her vulnerability, her body melted into the welcoming angles of his as if it were molten glass being poured into a mold of his making. Her pride dissolved into an agony of empty longing, and the words tumbled from her lips—not as the resounding accusation she'd intended to make, but as a plea for understanding. "I followed you because...because I saw you today—in the village with—with *her*." She paused to shore up the wispy strands of her voice. "And I had to... had to find out why."

He replied with silence. In the dark tunnel where servants had once scurried from one royal room to another, Monty waited with uncharacteristic patience for an answer she did not want to hear. And when she felt the warmth of his breath move downward to her ear, and then felt the nudge of his lips along the curve of her neck, she did not want to feel the liquid rush of her own surrender. She was a fighter. Crumbling at a man's touch was not her style. But the evidence was real and undeniable. Somehow, in some mystical way, Sebastian had claimed her and she supposed she would forever be his to command.

When he took her by the shoulders and turned her in his arms, she had no choice but to seek whatever fate he chose for her. His mouth captured hers in a crushing kiss, her arms slid around his waist to hold him fast and the embrace took on a will of its own, binding her to him, him to her, in a kiss that might have lasted a lifetime . . . or longer. Maybe she would die before the night was over, but she would die knowing that at least she was capable of loving without reason, capable of trusting without cause, capable of feeling emotions that until now hadn't existed in the world she knew.

He cupped her chin between his upraised palms, and as he pulled back reluctantly from the kiss, he continued to hold her face in the frame of his hands.

There wasn't enough light to provide a clear image, but Monty saw him with her heart and knew she was every bit as foolish as Lily de Vergille had been all those years ago. Like a hand in a glove, she fitted her courage around her wounded pride. "You used me," she challenged softly. "You used me to get to her."

The slight tension in his hands told her she'd struck a nerve, but to his credit he didn't try to deny the undeniable. "Yes," he said. "But all is not what it seems."

"Nothing is what it seems in this castle of illusions." She covered his hands with her own and felt his strength, his energy pulsating beneath her palms. Then she pulled away from temptation to face him in the dark passage. "I thought you were special, Seb. I thought you were different. I...I really thought something extraordinary was happening between us."

She sensed his movements in the darkness and then, as he switched on the beam, she saw that he had picked up the flashlight. The illumination revealed the taut pull of his jaw and the unsmiling set of his mouth. "Are you judge and jury, *ma fleur?* Am I to be condemned without a trial?"

Almost unconsciously, she began twisting the ruffled sleeve of her nightshirt. "The evidence is more than circumstantial. Sebastian, I saw you with her. You kissed her hand."

He nodded, the strange light creating a weird play of shadows across his face. Anyone else might have thought he looked sinister, but Monty felt her heart cramp with the artful attraction she saw instead.

"So you saw me with her. You saw me kiss her hand in greeting." He sounded as if he couldn't understand why she would mention the fact, as if he didn't perceive the reason she was upset. "Are you...jealous?"

As a green cow. But hurt, too—deeply, desperately hurt. "The point isn't how I feel. It's why I wasted any emotion at all on you. You're just like every other man.... Out for what you can get. And there's a lot to get from Montgomery Carlisle, isn't there? More riches than you could ever hope to acquire in your lifetime—in twenty lifetimes. I understand the lure of great wealth, and I understand your being tempted to romance her, Seb. But I'll never forgive you for using me to find out how best to do it.''

''I have not asked for your forgiveness.''

''No, but you asked for my help, didn't you? Gave me some cock-and-bull story about needing my assistance in finding your family's lost heritage. The heritage you lost is this château, isn't it? The reason you want Montgomery Carlisle is because she is your key to restoring your claim to this musty old throne. I see you for what you are, Sebastian. And believe me, Montgomery Carlisle isn't fooled by you, either.''

He wanted badly to contradict her, to tell her he knew exactly what Montgomery Carlisle thought of him and that he had known of her silly charade from the first moment. He wanted to defend himself against her accusations. But there was enough truth there to damn him to hell and back, and so he held his tongue and remained silent in the face of her suspicions.

She continued to vent her anger, letting it rise and flow over him like molten lava. And he told himself not to flinch. She did not understand his motives. She did not understand the very grave danger that stalked her. And she wouldn't listen, even if he forced her to hear the words. He was sorry—more sorry than she would ever know—that she had chosen to walk into the village this day. But how could he have guessed? And even if he had, it would not have changed his decision.

He knew he was not responsible for the accidents that had happened since her arrival at the château. And in his search for who might be accountable, it had seemed logical and necessary to talk with Eve. Unfortunately, she had been of little help. And now she was a weed growing crookedly and ugly in the garden he had planned to tend with such care.

Monty had seen him with her secretary and assumed the worst. If he offered reassurance, she would not believe him. If he confessed his knowledge of her true identity, she would, in all likelihood, turn away from him completely. Then, if another accident occurred, he would not be in a position to rescue her. He couldn't put her life in more danger. It was a risk his heart and his honor would not allow him to take. And so he kept quiet, stolidly accepting her accusations, aware of the deep pain he had so unintentionally caused her, aware of a painful ache that was all his own.

"May I have my flashlight now?" she asked when she ran out of anger.

He held it out to her. "May I ask of you one thing, *ma fleur?*"

"What is it?"

Her eyes looked enormous in the shaded light. And there was a distressing shimmer in their depths. He wanted to kiss away her fears, love away the insecurity and the loneliness she tried so hard to hide. "Trust me," he requested. "Trust me, *s'il vous plaît.*"

She hesitated. "Why should I? You have already betrayed me."

"Non." He shook his head, fighting the need to say more. "I ask simply and with my whole heart. Give me your trust. I have not and will not betray you."

For a moment, he thought she would refuse. But then he saw her desire to believe gather like a rainbow in her eyes, and his breath caught in his throat.

"If you're lying to me, Sebastian de Vergille, I will never, ever forgive you. And I'll do everything in my power to make you very, very sorry."

He caught her chin in his hand and moved swiftly to caress the indecision from her lips. "Is this a lie?" He returned to deepen the kiss, to seal the truth between them.

He took her hand and guided it to his chest, pressing her palm flat over the steady, rhythmic promise of his heartbeat. "Feel the racing of my heart?" he asked, his lips against her throat. "Is that a lie?"

He moved her hand down and over his stomach, then down farther to the irrefutable reality of his desire. "And is this, too, a lie?"

The tremor started deep within her.... Or perhaps it started in him. But the passion was suddenly vivid and bright and burning in the shadowy darkness, and he could not stop himself from jerking her into his arms.

Chapter Ten

If Edouard's ghost had happened to pass through the second-floor passageway at that moment, he would have turned a vaporous red in embarrassment—or a ghastly green with envy. Monty knew she should not allow Sebastian's kiss to ransack her dignity, knew she had every reason to mistrust his motives. But with his first touch, her body had turned traitor and the war was lost.

He pushed her back against the wall of the passageway and pinioned her there with a hand on either side of her body. His hips pressed against her with a demanding and obvious desire. His lips pulled and suckled her own with long, wet, hungry kisses.... Kisses that traveled to the base of her throat, wandered lower and lower and still lower, as the neck of her nightshirt parted and drifted downward to reveal first one creamy breast and then the other. And he took advantage, cupping her breast in one palm and kneading it with his fingers as he tongued the nubbed peak.

Flames of heady longing blazed inside her, and she laid her head against the dense wall at her back. Clinging to the solid strength of his arms, she raised one leg and ran her foot over the thick, rough texture of his dark jeans. She felt him tense, and a pleasant sense of power invaded her thoughts.

But he vanquished her illusions of control as he made a slow and devastating return trip from the valley of her breasts to the sloping hollows of her neck. Shivers cascaded over her, shivers so delicate they might have been woven of fine lace. In the chilly alcove of the tunnel, the blended heat of their bodies became a sensation in and of itself, and his need for her fused into her thoughts in an oddly frightening, wonderful way.

His lips traveled unhurriedly over the planes of her throat, along the sensitive skin below her chin, and teased her with nipping kisses all around her thirsty lips. He joined his hands with hers, tangling their fingers and creating a potent legacy of promise as he finally, thoroughly, and with a great degree of assurance, claimed her mouth as his own.

Her pride admitted she was no match for his seduction. Her reason gave up on any attempt to persuade her this might not be a wise course of action. Her body offered not a single sign of resistance to his determined progress. Not a solitary coherent thought challenged the waving white flag of her surrender.

Unless she counted the elusive remembrance of his voice saying, *Trust me. Trust me.*

Was there any alternative? Even without the sensual sabotage, she placed an enormous amount of trust in this man. He would prove worthy or not. She could do nothing to change the final consequence. But until such time as she knew beyond a doubt that he was undeserving of the trust she gave, she would believe in her own voice, believe in the judgment of her own heart against the caution of others. For this—this man, this moment, this miracle—was what she had always wanted, dreamed of, longed for. This was the love she'd thought did not, could not exist outside the pages of a book. This was the answer to a lifetime's worth of prayers.

Trust him? There was truly no other option.

She didn't care if Sebastian sheltered secrets behind the dark mystery of his eyes, beneath the shadowy expressions on his face. Undoubtedly, he did. But, then, she had a few secrets herself. Not the least of which was the fact that she was deeply, desperately in love with him. He parted her lips with his tongue, and she arched into him for the duration of the savage kiss. When the pressure eased, she eluded his mouth and pressed her lips against the wild, riotous pulse beating in the corded, vulnerable lines of his throat.

He shuddered at her touch, and she jeered at the thought that he could counterfeit such a spontaneous and telling response. Perhaps he didn't love her. Perhaps he was merely using her to service a need of his own. She didn't care. For now, he was hers in every way that mattered, and she would take from him until he had nothing left to give. And in the process, she would give back more than he had asked for and much, much more than he might have bargained for.

The idea released a ripple of pleasure inside her, and she curled her body around his like a cat seeking the caressing stroke of its master's hand. He was a concert of strength and lean masculinity, a powerful man brought into her arms through a deep and desperate need. She might not command him, but she could take his need into herself and fulfill it. Give and receive. Possess and surrender. Take the risk and trust him with her heart, her soul, the whole framework of her life.

Seb recaptured control, taking her mouth with a consuming kiss and probing the soft, sensuous lining of her lips with his tongue. The living ache of his desire was like a cup of boiling cider inside him, enticing him with its tangy scent, burning him at the first tempting taste. His need meshed with his reason like a strand of wire twisted into a soft, pliable surface. The threads of his passion cut through his best intentions.

He knew that Monty had not followed him with this result in mind. She had been angry, distrustful, hurt. She had intended to spy on him or to hunt him down and scald him with the venom of her anger. She had wanted to hear his denial, wanted him to admit his mistake. She hadn't meant to fall into his arms.

He knew that, and was certain his response would undermine whatever trust she had placed in him. But it was an honest response. He wanted her, needed her with a devastating hunger. And if she never understood his motivation, then he would live with that. She needed him, needed this confirmation of her own worth, needed to know that he made love to her because he wanted to and not because it would further his own cause.

Suddenly, everything became clear in his mind—how he would explain his actions; how he would assure her of the truth in his heart; how he would caress away her loneliness and help her find the love that awaited her in the haven of his embrace. And as her mouth opened under his, as her arms slipped up around his shoulders and her fingers wove into his hair, loosening it with a gentle tug, he knew the decision was made.

He would take what she offered, assuage both their needs, bury his fear for her safety in the dark caresses of the night. And if tomorrow she damned him, then he would know he had spent this time in heaven.

"Will you come with me?" he asked.

There was no hesitation in her whispered acquiescence, no swift questioning of where he meant to take her or what he meant to do. There was only trust—pure and guileless and honest. He felt honored and awed and burdened by the responsibility of that trust. Whatever happened, he would do his best to prove worthy.

He let his hands slide the length of her body as he stooped to pick up the fallen flashlight. He pressed the switch as he straightened, but the instrument was truly dead this time. Not a flicker of light came from it, no matter how he turned it, no matter what he tried. With a frown he was glad she could not see, he slipped the flashlight into his pocket.

"Take my hand." He held out his hand, and in the darkness her fingers slid confidently into his keeping.

He had learned much about the château's tunnels during the past few weeks and was confident he could navigate them in the dark. He would walk slowly, guide her safely through the labyrinth and tamp down the heady insistence of his desire until he reached the sanctuary of his bedroom. There he would love her. There he would give in to his physical need. There they would be safe in one another's arms.

But on the journey he would be on guard, vigilant against an unknown evil. He acknowledged his own inadequacies against that evil and hoped that no danger tracked Montgomery Carlisle this night.

Their passage was uneventful, marked only by the ragged anticipation of their breathing. He could feel the rapid beating of her pulse and was gratified to know that her desire for him hadn't been slackened by the delay. Building the fires of passion a second time would be a pleasure made more intense by the waiting, and his body ached with anticipation.

He opened the door to his bedroom—a much smaller, more humble room than her own—and stepped aside so that she could enter. Interest and curiosity were written across her expression as she walked from the darkness of the tunnel into the soft, muted light of the lantern that illuminated the room. But she turned immediately to him and lifted her shoulders in a coquettish shrug. Thus encouraged, the nightdress released its precarious hold and slithered to the floor. She stood before him naked and vulnerable and willing, offering her body to his, her heart for his taking.

He opened his arms and she walked into the sheltering circumference of his embrace. His pulse quickened to a fast two-step as she ran her hands up and over his shoulders and lifted her face for his kiss. As their lips touched with exquisite tenderness, the passion ignited and flared like a shooting star.

Under his palm, her skin was hot and as smooth as a lustrous pearl. Smooth, too, was the sweet pressure of her breasts rubbing against his chest, and he shifted his position in an effort to draw her closer. She pulled back slightly. With one hand she stroked the dark strands of his hair, freeing it to fall about his shoulders and face and with a slow, sensual motion. Her other hand dropped to the open neck of his shirt and slipped beneath the fabric.

He shivered at the intimacy of her touch, and what little control remained in him began a fast fade into the fierce urgency of possession. Her reactions were in marked contrast to his own—while he tried to curb his body's rush for satisfaction, to slow the lovemaking to a mutually gratifying pace, she grew bolder with each new advance. She seemed to take tremendous delight in working her delicate torture, and each time a sigh of ecstasy escaped his lips, she redoubled her effort. Her hand slid to his waist with private purpose, and he thought his heart might break a few ribs in its wild race of anticipation as she unfastened the top button of his jeans. If Monty hadn't had much practice at the art of seduction, she was one hell of a quick study.

He tried to restrain his body's response, but her hand was upon his most vulnerable part, and he groaned as he pushed her backward across the room and sent them both sprawling onto the bed. He pulled away only long enough to discard his clothes and to seek protection for her and for himself. Within moments he was as naked as she and his hands were exploring her with fevered haste. He wanted her to feel as he felt—hungry, empty and eager. He wanted to caress her, kiss her, possess her in such a way that she would never be able to erase these moments from her memory. Always, for the rest of her life, wherever she was, in whomever's arms she lay, she would have to recall this time, this wondrous feeling of oneness, this sultry, passionate and complete possession.

He tempted her with long, tender kisses, seduced her with singular attention to her most volatile pleasure points, worked her body until every response, every breath, every sweet moan that escaped her lips was orchestrated by his touch. The frenzied searching of her hands was his signal to shift her beneath him, part her legs and fulfill his commitment.

He entered her knowing he had limited time and control, but he was determined that his release would wait upon hers. Careful of her comfort, he rocked gently into her welcome heat and experienced the pain and exhilaration of withholding his own deliverance in deference to her enjoyment. When the convulsing wave of rescue surged around him, he heard her quickly indrawn breath of pleasured surprise and surged into her in an act of supreme and ultimate surrender.

For several long and honeyed moments, he hovered between the heaven of fulfillment and the satisfying afterglow of release. He rolled onto his side and enjoyed the simple pleasure of holding her close in his arms. She fit so perfectly against him, felt so right nestled in the angles of his body.

He was fast and fully in love with her—in love with Montgomery Carlisle. Helplessly entangled in all that she was and all that her future might be. Bound to her by events that had happened to other people in another century and yet had brought the two of them to this place and to this time. He loved her and he wanted only to be with her.... Whatever lies he might have told, whatever truths he had withheld and whatever she might choose to believe.

MONTY AWAKENED SLOWLY and realized she was in a strange room. The bed, too, was strange, not as soft nor as large as the one in her room, but it was wonderfully warm and comfortable. In fact, she couldn't remember the last time she'd felt so totally relaxed, so completely peaceful. She opened her eyelids and realized that Sebastian was sitting not far away in a large tapestry-covered chair. A pleasured warmth crept into her cheeks as she saw that he was watching her, and she wondered how long he had been doing so.

"Couldn't sleep?" she asked in a husky voice.

"I could not close my eyes when such beauty occupied my bed."

Monty's toes wiggled in unfettered delight. He had wanted to watch her as she slept. The idea seemed terribly private and deeply intimate. She had precious little experience for comparison, but she knew that no one, neither lover nor friend, had ever taken much pleasure in the simple act of looking at her—at least, no one had until now. She had lost her heart to Sebastian, but she was beginning to believe she had won a prize beyond measure.

"You couldn't think of anything better to do?"

A faint smile tucked in at the corners of his lips and he shook his head. "There was nothing I wanted to do more, *mon amour.*"

My love. He had called her his love. A wellspring of happiness fountained inside her heart. "You could have awakened me," she suggested.

Again, there was easy denial in the slight shake of his head. "The night has been perfect in every way."

For a moment his gaze clung to hers, made promises she locked away to take out and cherish later. "Perfect," she agreed with a secret smile.

"It is almost morning."

"No." She didn't want the sun to intrude, didn't want tomorrow to be here. "It is early, still."

His eyes darkened with tenderness. "I must take you back to your room before daylight. It is...safer that way."

She felt the nip of reality accompanied by a twinge of doubt and wondered fleetingly if he wanted to hide her presence in his room from someone...from *Eve*. But, no, Monty wouldn't withdraw her trust on such a flimsy possibility. She would grant him the benefit of her doubt and believe that his concern was for her. "All right," she said. "Give me a minute to find my clothes."

He stood and laid her rumpled nightshirt within her reach. There seemed no recourse except to take the gown, slip it over her arms and lace the front ties in a loose bow. She wanted to invite him to join her in the bed, wanted to feel his arms around her again, his lips against hers. But he seemed oddly distant as he slipped a pair of socks on her bare feet, draped a sweater around her shoulders for warmth and then opened the door of his room and waited for her to precede him into the darkness of the passageway beyond.

Sebastian didn't speak as he walked through the maze of tunnels, but he held on to her hand as if it were a king's ransom and he were the knight charged with its safekeeping. Quickly and efficiently, he led her back to the hidden panel that provided entry into her bedchamber. In a little over twenty minutes, Monty had gone from a warm bed to a cold one. She had gone from a feeling of shared love to wondering if she'd imagined the entire love scene. And because she couldn't find a better option, she clung to his promise. *Trust me,* he had asked of her. *I will not betray you.*

Seb kissed her, softly and with a tremendous degree of self-restraint, before he left without speaking a word of all the emotion that lay heavy upon his heart. What could he say? There was no way to explain—not yet. And so her questioning, lost look haunted him as he made his way back through the tunnel.

He was so deep within his own thoughts that he was only vaguely conscious of a voice, carried by echoes, elusive and intrusive in the cloistered passageway. But suddenly the sound registered and he stopped in his tracks to listen.

"I know what was *supposed* to happen." The voice rose with frustration, dropped abruptly into silence, then returned with a tense, softly threatening nuance. "I have done everything *exactly* as you said."

In the pause, Sebastian shifted position and focused his energy on determining where he was in the tunnel and where the sound might be coming from.

"That is not my fault!" Anger entered the voice along with a faint note of fear. A moment passed and then another, before the one-sided conversation continued. "How could I have known he would interfere?" The pause this time was barely noticeable. "Of course, I spoke to him. Do you think I'm an idiot?"

The ensuing silence palpated with tension. Sebastian looked around, trying still to discern the direction as well as the identity of the voice. But the tunnel had many twists and turns, and sound was easily distorted. It might have come from any one of the passageways or even from one of the rooms on the other side of the wall. He might be overhearing a telephone conversation or even a tête-à-tête in which the other person's voice was misdirected and out of range. The echo was too strong and the sound too deceptive to be sure.

"Yes, I understand...I *said,* I understand. There will be no more mistakes." The voice began to fade like a radio signal going out of range. "This time, she will die."

Will die... Will die... Will die...

The words seemed to bounce from wall to wall, floor to ceiling and back again, repeating the prophecy in an eerie repetition. A cold blast of air whipped around Seb's ankles and anchored him in a chill he couldn't shake. A chill rooted deep in fear.

If he had needed confirmation of his suspicions, he had it now, although he had precious little else. Monty was in mortal danger, and he didn't know when or how or from where it would come. He had asked her to trust him and she had. Now, if only he knew who wanted her dead and why, perhaps he could prove to her that her trust had not been misplaced.

With a weary and troubled frown, he turned and made his way back to the tunnel outside her bedchamber. He would keep vigil there, listening for the slightest noise, the least movement. In the days to come, he would keep her close, keep her unaware of the danger, and somehow he would keep her safe.

"THIS WILL BE the *jardins d'amour.*" Sebastian used sweeping hand gestures as he described his plans for the château gardens. "Each flower bed around the maze will be planted with yew and boxwood and will be trimmed in the shape of hearts and love knots. The lower level will consist entirely of a vegetable garden. We'll plant purple cabbages, a variety of fruits, golden pumpkins, red peppers, spinach, anything we want. It will be alive with color and texture at all seasons of the year."

Eve frowned as she looked at the overgrown and sketchy landscape, but Monty could imagine the neglected terraces taking shape, could see Seb's vision as if it were her own. She pointed to a sectioned-off area closer to the south tower. "And over there?"

"The herb garden. Charlotte insists I put it close to the kitchen."

"Do you honestly think she knows what to do with an herb, much less a whole plot of them?" Eve laughed a little at her own joke. "I keep hoping a bona fide chef will arrive to give her a few lessons. I'm beginning to have nightmares about her—" Eve wrinkled her nose in distaste "—fish stew."

Seb chuckled. "You don't think the dish has improved?"

"Not by a fish head."

Eve offered the rejoinder with a flirty smile, and Monty turned aside to look at the unkempt beauty of the maze. "Does Lily approve of your *jardins d'amour?*" she asked.

"I believe she would, yes," he replied.

"Who is Lily?" Eve demanded of Sebastian. "Can she cook?"

He shook his head. "Lily cannot leave the boundaries of the maze. She is doomed to haunt the place of her murder."

Eve shuddered. "In that case, you should tear down the maze and get rid of that ugly pavilion," Eve said, as if the idea had been on her mind for decades. "Then she'll leave. There are too many ghosts at the Château Carlisle as it is."

"Tearing down the maze will not free Lily's spirit, I'm afraid." Sebastian slipped his hands in his hip pockets. "Only an act of pure and unselfish love can do that." He lifted his shoulders in a slight shrug. "At least, that is what I've been told."

"I wouldn't have thought you'd believe in such nonsense, Sebastian."

Monty had to look at Eve to make sure that statement had come out of her mouth. "Aren't you the one who keeps spouting that nonsense about the Carlisle curse?"

Eve smiled with rare good humor and touched Sebastian's arm. "Don't pay any attention to her. I don't think she got enough sleep last night."

Monty's gaze winged directly to Seb's and shared the memory of last night's intimacy. The irritation that had just begun to nibble at her composure wilted like a hothouse bloom in an early frost. She had spent the past two nights enjoying some very basic pleasures in Sebastian's bed while Eve had slept alone. Monty could find room in her heart to feel a little sorry for her secretary, but she had no reason to be jealous of her.

Trust me, Sebastian had requested. And for two beautiful days and two long, passion-filled nights since he'd spoken those words, Monty had put the questions out of her mind. At night she had gone with Seb through the tunnels, helped him in his search to find a way around the secret and sealed entrance to the south tower, believed him when he said all he sought was the de Vergille chalice. And each night, the search had ended in his bedroom as she followed her heart into his arms, gave her body up to his sweet possession. The treasure they had found was that of long, uncomplicated conversation and the mystical power of love shared. Monty was content. *Trust me,* he had said. She was very sure she had made the right choice.

"Really, Seb..." Eve pursued the subject of Lily's maze with a critical eye. "Don't you think your garden would fare better if the maze and the ghost were gone? Why preserve the scene of a murder in the middle of your *jardins d'amour?*"

Seb looked back at the maze with an expression of dark affection. "Love has many faces, does it not, *mademoiselle?*"

"Miss Carlisle! Miss Carlisle!" The summons came from the château, from one of the windows on the second floor, from a robust Charlotte who was leaning half in and half out of the window. "They're here."

"They're here?" Monty murmured under her breath as she looked toward the château and the unmistakable sight of Charlotte's cobweb white hair.

"Now what is she yelling about?" With a cool, quick frown, Eve assumed the role of Montgomery Carlisle, which seemed to be an easier fit each time she donned it. "I'll go and see why she has to shout like a commoner instead of walking out here in a civilized manner to tell me whatever it is she—"

The words trailed away like the tail of a comet and Monty's throat went dry with just one look at Eve's thunderstruck expression. She turned to follow Eve's gaze and her heart beat a quick protest as she stared at the two men and two women who were walking down the wide steps of the château and moving like prize pedigreed cats toward the gardens.

"Monty?" One of the women lifted her hand in a yoo-hoo kind of wave. "Monty! We're here! We're here to celebrate your birthday with you."

"I-i-it's Edwin, Aunt Josephine, Cousin Sophie and her f-f-fiancé." Like a clown stripped of face paint, Eve lost any resemblance to her alter ego. She seemed suddenly anxious as she turned a guilty gaze on Monty. "Wh-wh-what are they doing here?"

"I was just getting ready to ask you the same question."

Eve pursed her lips in a stubborn line. "I g-guess they didn't want you to be alone on your birthday."

Rebellion welled like Old Faithful inside her, but Monty struggled with—and won—the right perspective. Celebrate her birthday? Not likely. The whole clan was here to keep an eye on her and that could only mean that Eve had faithfully reported everything to them.

"You're behind this, aren't you?" Monty shot a sideways glance at Eve and received a smug look in return.

Sebastian was conscious of the frozen silence that fell like snow over his garden, and he was well aware of the unspoken but glaring conversation going on between Monty and her secretary. He didn't recognize the visitors, but it was obvious they were Monty's family, and it was just as obvious that she did not want them here. And then he recalled the charade. Monty's little masquerade as an ordinary person was about to be uncovered.... And Sebastian realized he was about to find himself in a world of trouble.

The newcomers approached like the Four Horsemen, and Seb clung to a last and desperate hope that Monty could avert the catastrophe heading his way. But it was soon obvious that there was nothing anyone could do. The aunt and cousin stepped forward to embrace—and corner—Monty with expansive smiles. The older blonde grasped Monty by the shoulders and executed a quick one-two, cheek-to-cheek greeting. "Montgomery, dear, how lovely to see you. You're looking a bit flushed. Should you be outside in this damp air?"

"I'm surprised your allergies haven't been getting the best of you." The second woman was a younger version of the first—pale, pretty and plastic. Her party-pink perfectly-shaped fingernails contrasted with the sunflower yellow of Monty's sweater. "The château must have eleven million different molds growing inside. Why, I nearly sneezed my head off. And out here, the pollen must be as thick as San Francisco fog." She threw a smile over her shoulder at the man with the thin mustache. "Monty, you remember my fiancé, Milton, of course."

"Of course," Monty said automatically. "How are you, Milton? And Edwin, I am happy to see you."

The older man was a shorter version of Orson Welles, and his voice was deep and confidence inspiring. "I thought you might be."

"Don't be silly, Edwin," the older woman said. "She's happy to see all of us, aren't you, Monty? You don't have to pretend you liked being in this haunted villa with no one to talk to except the staff."

Both women gave Sebastian an assessing glance, then each in turn nodded politely to Eve. "Hello, Miss O'Halloran," the older woman said. "Are you enjoying your visit to our little château on the Loire?"

Eve's cheeks flamed a bright, embarrassed red, and she turned to Monty with a look of terrible contrition. "I g-guess I should have mentioned...should have told them that you and I...that w-we were pretending to be each other."

Sebastian's heart sank like a stone. He had expected introductions all around, had thought he would have at least a minute or two to figure out what his reaction to this revelation should be. But the situation had taken a broad leap from bad to worse and he was facing disaster, toe-to-toe.

To her credit, Monty confronted the deadlock with a fatalistic shrug. "What a...pleasant surprise. And how thoughtful of you to make such a long trip just so I wouldn't have to spend my birthday alone."

The older woman's expression turned somber. "This is no time for you to be by yourself, dear. You know how I worry about you. Especially with that awful *curse* hanging over your head like the sword of Damocles. I just couldn't bear to think of you facing this birthday without your family's support and protection."

"Now, Monty..." The older gentleman stepped forward with a kind smile and a voice of authority. "What is this about you and Miss O'Halloran 'pretending to be each other'?" His laughter was deep with affectionate indulgence. "You haven't been playing games with the staff now, have you?"

Sebastian thought Monty looked a little green, but he admired the way she squared her shoulders and faced the music. "There isn't a staff, per se, Edwin, but allow me to introduce Sebastian de Vergille, the gardener."

Edwin's handshake was full, firm and indifferent. "From the looks of the place, you've been doing some digging in the dirt. Monty wasn't out here pretending she knew anything about gardening, was she?"

His laughter encouraged the others to join him in the amusing idea. It also announced, clearly and concisely, that Montgomery Carlisle didn't dig in the dirt and that no one of any intelligence would mistake Monty for anything but what she was—a pampered American princess.

"What a clever scam, cousin." Sophie showed a mouthful of perfect teeth to Monty as she slipped her hand through the crook of Milton's arm. "Pretending to be your own *secretary*. Sometimes you have just the wildest ideas." She fastened a curious, Barbie-doll smile on Sebastian. "I'm Monty's cousin, Sophie."

Sebastian reluctantly gave her the response she so obviously sought.... A courteous and subservient bow. *"Mademoiselle,"* he said. "Welcome to France and to the Château Carlisle."

"Why, you speak perfect English." Her laughter was a little trill of delight. "I can see why Monty might want to meet you on more...equal ground. Be honest, though, you were never fooled by my cousin's masquerade, were you, Sebastian?"

Doomed. Seb could almost hear the snap of the trap as it closed on him. Lying now would only save him for the moment and would likely result in him being caught in a bigger and better trap later. He forced a smile and hoped Monty would believe he was bluffing. "It would be difficult to mistake Mademoiselle Carlisle for anyone other than a wealthy American."

"She's always been a clever little thing, always been eager to test the social limits." Sophie tossed Monty a smile as she might toss a bone to a favorite Pekingese. "But she just can't be trusted to know which ideas would be better left to die a natural death. She keeps us entertained, I'll tell you." Sophie shook her head. "But I'm glad to know she didn't fool you, Sebastian. Playing games with her gardener is a bit, uh, lowbrow, if you know what I mean."

He felt Monty's gaze, sensed her anger and her underlying indecision. He didn't know if the anger was directed at him, but he was fairly certain the indecision was. She was beginning to question him, beginning to analyze all that had happened to see if it were possible for him to have known. Now seemed like a good time to change the subject. "Will you be stay—"

"You did know all along, didn't you?" Eve's voice sounded like a dog's squeaky toy, and Seb restrained a groan at her interruption. "You knew. Of course, you knew." She whirled on Monty. "The joke is on us, this time, Miss Carlisle. I did just what you said, tried to act like I thought you would, and he knew who was who from the first moment he laid eyes on us. But then, you probably knew that he knew." The curve of

Eve's lips quivered and her eyes glistened with unshed tears. "Well ... Imagine my embarrassment."

She turned and walked quickly back to the château.

Sophie watched her go. "What an odd little person. Wherever did you find her, Edwin?"

"An agency, I believe." Edwin didn't even glance at Eve's humiliated retreat. "Monty likes her," he said, as if that closed the matter. "Now, Sebastian, could I have a few moments of your time? There's a matter—" he glanced at the women, then lowered his voice "—a rather delicate matter, regarding the caretaker, which I would like to discuss with you. Is there some private place where we might talk?"

Sebastian could tell by the calculation in Monty's gaze, by the tight line of her chin, that she would have liked to have a few words with him in private as well. She had made her choice. He could see the light of battle in her eyes and knew she had chosen to believe in his guilt. He wasn't surprised when she turned her back on him.

"Aunt Jo. Sophie," she said. "Let's go inside. It's gotten unpleasantly chilly here in the *jardins d'amour.*"

The garden of love was quickly becoming a jungle of misconceptions, Seb thought. And he was as guilty of deceit as anyone else. Of necessity, Monty stepped close to him as her aunt and cousin preceded her on the path from the gardens to the château. But she didn't look at him, didn't touch him, didn't act as if anything were wrong. But when she walked past him, her gaze collided with his for an instant and he saw the disillusionment and the fury in her eyes.

"Trust me." She mouthed the words in such a way that only he could see her disgust for them. Then, with the slightest disbelieving shake of her head, she tossed her hair back from her face and walked away.

Sebastian realized he had no defense. She wasn't going to listen to him a second time. Running deeper than her faith and feelings for him, her own insecurity was now his worst enemy. He was going to have to climb the mountain of her doubt to declare that he loved her. But saying so was one thing, proving he meant it, quite another.

And he could see that protecting Monty from the Carlisle curse had now become a Herculean task.

Chapter Eleven

Silence filled the tunnel with a cloying presence as the flashlight beam pushed stubbornly at the darkness, eking out a path to Monty's bedroom. For the first time in all his excursions through the château, Sebastian was afraid. Fear edged his senses with an uncertain alarm, and he moved stealthily, steadily through the passageway, listening, looking, careful of the noise he himself might make.

His plan was simple. He would talk with Monty if she were still awake, force her to face the danger he saw so clearly, the danger that ached in his consciousness as if it were a broken bone. He had to make her understand, and if she wouldn't he would stand ready to protect her, no matter what her opinion of him.

And if she were already asleep?

Then he would stand vigil beside the hidden door, ready to protect and defend her with his whole heart and soul, his body and his brain. The plan was simple, certainly, but what it lacked in finesse, he would make up for in tenacity. No one was going to hurt Monty while he could prevent it.

A gust of wind whirled past. Whispers of sound flew like bats over his head. He sensed a movement behind him, ducked, but too late.

Sebastian never knew what hit him.

SHE EXPECTED HIM TO come to her, and despite the ache of betrayal in her heart, she wanted to see him. He would lie to her, she knew that. Just as he had lied before. *Mon amour,* he had called her. My love. But she wasn't his love. He loved the things her money could buy...the château, to name only one. Of course he had known her identity all along. There had been plenty of clues, if she had but allowed herself to see them. Now that she had had a chance to reflect on all the time they'd spent together, she realized he had to have known.

He never called her by name. *Petite fleur. Ma fleur.* Terms of endearment that now seemed like red flags of warning. He had led her to reveal information about Montgomery Carlisle, and he had fed her the information he wanted her to have. Oh, it was all very clear from the vantage point of her new perspective.

She had been blind to believe, stupid to trust, silly to think she could escape the specter of her fortune...even for a few days of pretense. The only hope she nurtured now was that Sebastian truly meant her no harm. And when he came to her room tonight, as she was certain he would, she would find out if that hope, too, was a foolish one.

A noise at the door of the adjoining room pulled Monty's attention. She had asked Eve to stand guard there and to scream bloody murder if she heard anything suspicious. Another bit of silliness on her part, Monty thought. What good would Eve be in an emergency? She'd probably faint dead away.... Without uttering so much as a squeak of protest.

Monty was surprised and a little annoyed when the latch clicked and Eve stepped through the doorway into Monty's room. Outside, lightning flashed across the pewter sky and reflected like a jagged crack in the myriad panes of window glass. Eve turned her head to look out, and Monty wondered if she was investigating the sound of thunder.

"Come over here," Eve said.

Monty rather liked the idea of being in bed when Seb arrived. She wanted to be sitting in bed, reading an inspirational book, as if she hadn't given him or his betrayal a second thought. She didn't want him to think she expected his visit or that he might be invited into her bed. To that end, she was still in the silk slacks and blouse she'd worn to dinner.

A real dinner, served in full light, courtesy of a real electrician who had restored power to the château in a matter of thirty minutes. A real dinner, prepared by the real chef Edwin had brought with him, served by two female staff members, who had been hired and brought along as well. Edwin's middle name was efficiency, and he'd already set about rectifying problems at the château. Sebastian hadn't joined them for dinner, but as Aunt Jo and Sophie had been prompt to point out, he was merely the gardener. What had happened to Louis and Charlotte, Monty could only guess. She hadn't seen them since her family's arrival, which was probably just as well. Edwin was always right about employees, and if he'd fired Louis and his wife, she'd really rather not know the circumstances.

"Come over here," Eve repeated in a tone that was unusually sharp.

"What for?" Monty pushed aside the bed covers and swung her feet over the side of the mattress. "Is there something outside? In the garden?"

"Yes." Eve moved to the French doors and opened them, allowing the storm to sweep into the room much as it had on the night of their arrival at the château, billowing the sheer curtains, twisting its chilly fingers into the loose tendrils of Monty's hair. "There's a light," Eve continued. "Inside the maze."

Monty approached the open windows as Eve walked out onto the balcony. "There." Eve pointed into the darkness. "Do you see it?"

With her first step over the threshold, Monty felt the touch of a misty rain on her cheek and the sudden, certain sense that she was in danger. "I can't see anything through the rain."

The wind whipped Eve's brown hair into a frenzy, and when she turned toward Monty it covered her face, concealing her expression. She lifted a hand to sweep it out of her way, and that's when Monty saw the gun—a short, shiny pistol glinting an ugly, imminent threat.

"Put that down, Eve."

With a glance at the cold steel in her hand, Eve shrugged. "Sometimes these things fire accidentally, you know."

Fear laid a death grip on Monty's heart. "Eve?" she whispered in a plea for reassurance.... A prayer that she wasn't facing yet another person who was about to betray her. "No...Oh, Eve, no."

A glint of madness flickered deep in Eve's eyes as she slicked her rain-dampened hair back from her forehead. But it wasn't the madness, the touch of insanity, that Monty feared most. It was the unfettered gleam of jealousy and undiluted hatred.

"You thought you were clever, didn't you?" Eve's smile was pure sunshine. Her voice was calm, collected, completely steady. "Switching identities with me. Becoming poor, little Eve O'Halloran just so you could enjoy the novelty of being *ordinary*. Bestowing your royal crown on me as if you were the princess and I were the queen of the damned. It never occurred to you that I was behind the accidents, did it?" She clicked her tongue in mild chastisement. "All but the angel. That *was* an accident, a little omen of things to come. But it was me that night in the tunnel. I pushed you down the stairs. Unfortunately, I didn't wait to make sure you'd fallen all the way down. Then, in

Paris, I waited outside the bookstore for hours, watching for you, watching for my opportunity. But you were lucky again and escaped without a scratch.''

Eve shook her head sadly. ''Seb's BMW wasn't so lucky, though. I was afraid he would notice the marks and be suspicious of me. But then, while I was trying to buff out the scratches, I realized that if you saw the car, saw the marks on the hood, you'd believe Sebastian was behind the accidents and turn against him, leaving yourself more vulnerable than before. It was a perfect opportunity, and that silly caretaker played his part to perfection.''

''Louis?'' Monty swallowed hard. ''Louis helped you?''

''Not intentionally, no, but as you're just finding out, Monty, anyone can be manipulated. All I had to do was open the garage doors and prop open the tunnel door so that when it was pushed, it would swing back with a bit of force. That worked even better than I dreamed it would.'' The curve of her lips was self-satisfied and evil. ''And you didn't think I was smart enough to fool anybody, did you? You never once thought I could be anything other than your meek, little secretary. Well, the joke's on you, Miss Carlisle. You made it all so easy. Too easy, really. If you hadn't been so lucky, you'd be dead already and this last bit of theatrics wouldn't be necessary.''

She waved the gun, bringing it up and under Monty's left breast, pressing the muzzle into the soft, vulnerable silk and holding it there against the steady pulsing of her heart. "You have been incredibly lucky. But no one, not even the princess, gets lucky every time."

"Why are you doing this?" Monty's voice was full of a pain too deep for tears. "Tell me what I've done to make you hate me?"

"You were born. Born into the lap of luxury, silver spoon, golden scepter, crown jewels and all. Montgomery Carlisle, the last heir to a fortune bigger than the U.S. treasury. And I was born with nothing. Life isn't fair, but then I guess you wouldn't know about that, would you, Miss Carlisle?"

The knot in her throat was raw, agonizing emotion, and Monty couldn't have forced a word past it if she'd been able to think of one. Life was not fair. She'd agree with Eve on that one.

"Don't look so sad." Eve applied a steady pressure and the gun muzzle pushed a little deeper into Monty's skin. "The accident will be over in less than a minute. With a little luck, you won't even feel any pain."

She took a step forward and Monty was forced to step back. "I'll discover your body," Eve continued. "I must have heard you scream. Or maybe I was awakened by the wind coming through the windows you so carelessly opened. Such a tragic fall. I'll be reduced to stammering grief for the inquest, but I'll be able to tell the officials that I had begged you to stay off the balcony. Even Sebastian told you the first night we arrived that it wasn't safe. And there will be any number of people who can testify that you delight in defying sensible, sane advice.''

With her next backward step, Monty glanced over her shoulder and discovered how very small the balcony actually was. Her voice escaped its prison on a raspy breath. ''What can you hope to gain by my murder, Eve? You won't get away with it. Edwin and Aunt Jo are here at the château. You'll be the first person they suspect.''

Eve's smile was slyly indulgent. ''Sebastian will be the murderer, *ma fleur*. He's the perfect suspect. Why his own great-grandmother was murdered by your great-grandfather. You own the château that should have been his birthright. That's a pretty solid motive by any standards. And I, of course, will testify that I begged you not to trust him.'' The gun made another jab into Monty's flesh. ''But, alas, you told me to mind my own business. What could I do? I get paid to do what I'm told.''

Monty saw the truth then, felt the stab of its knife through her heart, tasted its bitter flavor in her mouth. ''That's it, isn't it? You're being paid to commit murder. Don't be foolish, Eve. Don't risk your future for a reason as pathetically empty as money.''

Eve's smile tightened. ''A lot you'd know about that. A pampered, spoiled little princess who has never gone without the luxuries of life, much less the basics. Don't kid yourself. You don't know the first thing about emptiness.''

Oh, but she did. She knew firsthand about emptiness and loneliness and betrayals. "Don't risk your chance to have a future, Eve. Please, listen to me."

"Unless you go over that wall, I don't have a future." She pulled back the hammer of the gun, and Monty moved instinctively away and felt the bite of the cold, wet railing slice across her buttocks.

"You've reached the end of the fairy tale, Montgomery." Eve placed her free hand on Monty's shoulder. "I warned you to be careful. I tried to tell you the Carlisle curse was real. You remember the curse, don't you? I know, technically we're a bit early. You're not supposed to die until the eve of your twenty-seventh birthday. But I couldn't wait until midnight." She smiled in pure delight. "So, sue me."

As the pressure against her shoulder increased, Monty couldn't seem to move, could feel her center of gravity shift backward, out over the railing, and all she could think of was that stupid and oft-repeated Carlisle curse—*The last heir of Josiah Carlisle will die...last heir...will die...will die...will die... will...die...will...*

"Monty! Grab the gun! Fight. Don't die...don't die..."

Sebastian's voice echoed faint and far away, but Monty rallied to the call. Anger rose like a phoenix from her fear, strength flowed through limbs too numb and weak to resist. Her fingers left the slippery security of the railing and wrapped like claws around Eve's hand, clamping around the barrel of the gun and pushing back at the same time. The gun muzzle snagged her blouse but lost its sure aim at her heart.

"Stop it!" Eve demanded, as if she couldn't believe Monty would put up a fight. "Let go! I said, let go!"

Monty's attention was securely fastened on the gun and how she could get it away from Eve. As the struggle intensified, Monty pushed the muzzle to one side, away from her body, and used every ounce of strength she possessed to pull the gun away from Eve.

Realizing that losing the gun was tantamount to losing the war, Eve held on with sheer, dogged determination, and the two of them strained to retain control, pulling one against the other, the gun was like a bone of contention between them.

"Let go!" Eve yanked on the handle and Monty slipped on the wet balcony. The gun slid across her palms and out of her grasp, exploding upward into the storm, an explosion of fire and noise that echoed like thunder through the night. Startled by the shot and thrown off-balance by the sudden release, Eve stumbled backward, hit the rail and fell backward over the balcony with only one long, furious scream to mark her passage.

Monty made a futile grab at the empty air, as if she could turn back time and keep Eve from falling. On legs that trembled like a newborn foal's, she moved to the railing and looked over. A flash of lightning revealed Eve's crumpled body four floors below, sprawled on the terrace in a twisted, lifeless pattern.

"Eve!" Monty screamed in denial, but not a breath of sound broke the deadly silence. Her knees gave way and she sank to the balcony floor, quivering like a lost child. The rain covered her in a sheet of windblown cold and she sat frozen, too weak even to wrap her arms around herself in a shallow attempt at comfort.

"Monty! Monty, are you all right?" Sebastian appeared on the balcony, his concern pouring over her in a wave of fluid French. His hands reached for her and drew her up out of the rain and into his arms. "Were you shot?" he asked. "Are you hurt?"

Monty shook her head, hoping to stifle the riot of words inside the vacuum of silence that was her brain. With perfect weariness, she laid her head against his shoulder and absorbed the rapid-fire pounding of his heart. Her own heart couldn't seem to find its rhythm, couldn't seem to understand that the danger was past.

Seb drew her back, off the balcony and into the sanctuary of the bedchamber. He held her, safe, treasured and warm in his embrace. His hand was a stroke of solace in her hair. His arms were an asylum. The heat of his body was a blanket against the cold. The soft, ceaseless, comforting murmur of his voice was all she needed to know of heaven.

It's over. It's done. You're safe. Safe. Monty drank in the words he crooned to her, as if she had been given a chalice full of wine to quench her agonizing thirst. Eve had fallen. The gun was lying, spent and useless, somewhere outside in the rain. But she was safe. And Seb was here.

Sounds began to register—the banging of a door thrown open in haste, the indistinct and definite noise of movement nearby, the echo of voices raised in alarm. A tremor shook her from head to toe as reality pinched and fractured her moment of peace.

"What happened? Did I hear a gunshot? Eve, where is Mont—?" The light was switched on as Edwin burst into the room like a bat out of hell, followed by a rattled and winded Aunt Jo. "Monty," he said. "Are you . . . ? Is everything all right?"

She turned to face the only family she knew, and Sebastian's arm tightened around her shoulder. With more reluctance than she allowed herself to show, she shrugged free of his support. Real life, she thought, had to be faced alone.

"I'm all right, Edwin." Her voice was a shadow, a ghostly whisper in the suddenly still room. "Eve tried to push me over the balcony ledge."

"Eve?" Aunt Jo's confusion was immediate, her distress obvious, as her gaze canvassed the scene like a lighthouse beacon, slashing the darkness in search of ships in peril. "Where is Eve?"

Monty swallowed over the dryness in her throat. "She . . . She fell. I don't think there—there's any hope that she survived."

Edwin hurried past the open windows, the fluttering curtains, and moved onto the rain-swept balcony. He leaned over the railing to look down at the terrace below. Lightning streaked the sky in a jagged flash, and a jolting crack of thunder followed a moment later. "She's dead. Probably broke her neck and died instantly," Edwin announced as he walked back into the bedchamber and closed the balcony doors. "I heard a gunshot. Did you shoot her?" He turned the question quickly and purposefully on Sebastian.

"Eve tried to push Monty from the ledge. They struggled. The gun fired into the air. Eve lost her balance and fell over the edge." Sebastian explained quickly, neatly, tying up the events into a concise, cold-blooded package. "I entered the room just as the gun went off. No one could have saved her."

"That isn't entirely true, Seb." Monty lifted her chin, squared her shoulders. "She could have been saved. That's the real tragedy."

Edwin took a step forward, his hand reaching for Monty in a gesture of sympathy. "Don't blame yourself, dear. She was insane, greedy. She doesn't deserve your compassion, and there's no reason for you to feel any guilt at her death. I know this is a painful, unfortunate experience, but it is not your fault."

Monty nodded. "I can't escape my share of the blame, Edwin. I didn't see what was going on right under my nose. I should have been more aware, more suspicious, and because I wasn't, an innocent young woman has died."

"Monty, dear." In a flutter of satin negligee, Aunt Josephine moved to join the small circle around Monty. "Don't be silly. Miss O'Halloran was obviously unstable. Mentally imbalanced. The sort of person Edwin and I have always tried to keep out of your life. If anyone is at fault, it is the two of us. We should have been more selective in choosing a companion for you."

"Oh, I believe you selected Eve very carefully, Aunt Jo. I believe you and Edwin hired her to kill me."

"That's nonsense, Montgomery." Edwin's denial exploded in anger. "If anyone means you harm, it's the staff I so carelessly hired long-distance to run this château." His furious gaze singled out Sebastian. "Ask your gardener what is really going on around here. Ask him what his interest in the château is."

She turned then to look at Seb, noticed his disheveled and matted hair, saw the unnatural color in his face, the tinge of pain in his dark, dilated pupils. "Seb?" she questioned softly. "What happened to you?"

"Someone struck me from behind in the tunnel," he answered. "I was coming here to talk to you when I was knocked unconscious."

Monty gathered the information and turned it back toward Edwin. "Were you afraid Seb would rescue me? Did you intend to kill him, too?"

"You're being stupid, Monty. He was coming to make sure you went over the balcony. If we hadn't come in just now—"

"If you hadn't come in just now, Edwin, I might have believed you weren't involved. But your response was too quick, a bit too practiced. You and Aunt Jo came in here expecting to find Eve, expecting that my body would be the one lying twisted and lifeless on the terrace.''

"We heard a gunshot," Edwin stated impatiently.

"You couldn't have heard it, Edwin. With the storm, the rain, the sheer thickness of the walls, you couldn't possibly have heard the sound of a single shot from a small pistol. And you got here too quickly. You had to have been waiting in Eve's room, waiting for the signal that the final 'accident' had occurred."

"Monty!" Aunt Jo's voice was full of horror. "You've gone mad. I have no reason to want you dead. I'm your family. I love you. Haven't I raised you and treated you like my own daughter?"

"I thought you had, Aunt Jo. But then you and Edwin insisted on sending me here in secret, without a word to my friends or anyone else about where I would be staying. I was told it was because Stanton Grainger was threatening legal action over the bet I made with him, but I could have gone anywhere, in or out of the country, until he calmed down. And the truth is, I didn't need to run and hide. I wanted to give him the Carlisle Ruby. But, Edwin, you advised me to hide out in France, in a deserted château with a meager staff, no electricity and no companions except Eve, the one you chose for me. Was it just a coincidence that the château came equipped with dark passageways, a ghostly history and secrets of its own?"

"We wanted to protect you," Aunt Jo protested. "We were afraid for you, Monty. Your birthday is only a day away. Your *twenty-seventh* birthday."

Monty nodded, becoming more sure of herself with every twist of the conversation. "Ah, yes. The Carlisle curse. The one you've been telling me about over and over again these past few months. Twenty-seven, the magical age at which my trust is to be distributed, the age when the responsibility of managing the Carlisle fortune becomes mine to oversee. A rather suspicious time for a curse to take effect, isn't it?"

"You are obviously upset by the accident, Montgomery." Edwin assumed a stance of authority, a tone of command. "There is no need to insult your aunt and me in this fashion. You have absolutely no basis for these accusations."

"Perhaps I can provide one." Sebastian moved, positioning his body protectively beside Monty. "Greed. You have betrayed Monty out of greed. She cares but little for the treasures accumulated by her ancestors, but you..." He shared his condemning stare between Monty's aunt and uncle. "You saw the opportunity to secure more of her fortune for yourselves and for your own daughter, Sophie, by selling paintings, tapestries, furniture, anything of value. You chose items that could be easily reproduced, if they couldn't just vanish outright, and you chose things that Monty would never notice. You were so sure of her inattention and of her complete trust in you, that you didn't hesitate to send her here, where you've stolen nearly everything of value, stripping the château of its history as well as its riches."

Edwin's jaw clenched with his tension. "You're a long way from the gardens, Seb, but don't think I can't bury you with a slander suit."

"The treasures of the château have been disappearing steadily over the past several years. Louis asked me to verify his suspicions because of my personal history and knowledge of the château. A few days ago, we received confirmation of the sale of château property through an antique dealer in London. It is only a matter of time before the trail leads to you, *monsieur*, only a matter of a week or two before you will be forced to answer for your management of Monty's trust."

Aunt Jo was the weak link and with one unguarded look at Edwin, she revealed the validity of the accusations and wiped the shred of remaining doubt from Monty's heart. For the second time that night, she tasted the bitterness of betrayal. "The Carlisle Ruby was part of it, wasn't it?" she asked, seeing the truth emerge like the lost piece of a puzzle coming to light and fitting exactly into place. "When I lost the bet to Stanton and asked for the Carlisle Ruby, you knew he'd have it appraised and discover it was a reproduction of the original, a worthless replica of Joan of Arc's fabled ruby. Did you make up that particular myth, too, Aunt Jo?" She lifted her hand to preclude any protest. "It doesn't matter. The point is, you panicked and decided that the infamous Carlisle curse should come to pass."

Monty shook her head with immeasurable sadness. "You know, Edwin, I wouldn't have known. I care so little about the jewels that if you'd said the ruby had been nothing more than a colored stone all along, I'd have believed you. I wouldn't have even questioned you. I'd have teased Stanton and made some other silly bet with him, and the ruby would have been forgotten." She swallowed hard, feeling the trauma of the night seep into her soul like an icy, overwhelming darkness. "And if you'd asked, I would have given you anything I owned, anything at all."

Edwin stood stiffly and with unforgiving composure. Aunt Jo began to cry. "You can't believe we meant to harm you," she began to protest, but Edwin stopped her with a touch.

"Say nothing," he commanded. "Monty will have to prove her outlandish claims in an American court. We won't dignify her accusations with denials."

Monty sheltered her grief by turning aside. Sebastian placed his hand on her shoulder. "Louis found me unconscious in the tunnel, and we knew the attempt on your life would be made tonight. He and Charlotte have gone for the authorities and should return very soon, but Eve's accident must be reported right away. If you wish, I will handle the matter for you." He squeezed her shoulder reassuringly. "You can trust me," he said.

"Yes," she whispered, her strength vanished along with her ability to face the emptiness in her heart. Later, she would learn to handle details. Later, she

would take charge of her own destiny and the respon-
sibilities of the Carlisle name. Later, she would manage her life without assistance from people who said
trust me. But this one last time, she would allow
someone else to take care of the unpleasant tasks.

She nodded. "Please, Seb. Do whatever is necessary."

MONTY SAT ON THE broken step of the pavilion and
wished Lily's ghost would come and talk with her. Lily
had been a mother, once. Surely in the afterlife she still
possessed some element of that maternal and comforting presence. It was possible her spirit would have
understanding and sympathy to offer the shambles
that was all that remained of Monty's heart.

She had never been so alone. Now there really was
no one. No family. No friends. Not even a hired companion. Sophie had dissolved in a fit of tears, clinging to Milt's arm and casting condemning glances in
Monty's direction. She could have been a party to the
thefts. She might have known about the murder plot,
but Monty didn't think so. She thought Sophie, like
herself, was a victim of the Carlisle fortune.

The money. It always came back to the money. How
many people would believe that a fortune the size of
hers could be a curse? That a few family heirlooms,
acquired a century or more ago, could cause the de-
struction of a family and the death of a misguided
young woman.

From the recesses of the past, Monty tried to remember the day Aunt Josephine and her husband, Edwin, had arrived in her life. She'd later learned that had been the day of her parents' funeral, but her only memory was of the big stuffed bear Aunt Jo had thrust into her arms. Monty hadn't really liked the bear, but had thought it would be rude to say so. A toy was no substitute for the arms of a living, breathing parent. But Aunt Jo had meant well. Monty had always believed that. Now, she supposed, every memory, every action, every spoken declaration of affection would have to be called up, reexamined, labeled anew as the lie it was.

A breath of wind ruffled the overgrown limbs of the maze, and shivering, Monty rubbed the chill from her upper arms. She waited for Seb, knowing he would find her here. She knew, too, what he was going to say, how he would confess his love for her, swear his undying devotion.

Looking up at the turrets of the château, Monty allowed her lips a bittersweet smile. His devotion was rooted in the château. It was the home of his ancestors. His history went back much further than hers. The Carlisles had caused only trouble to the de Vergille family. And whether or not Seb had any true feelings of affection for her, Monty knew he would do anything, say whatever was necessary, to get his history back. She knew that with certainty, even if he did not.

She wasn't looking forward to this confrontation. She didn't want to hear him speak words of love and commitment. She couldn't live with him and forever wonder if he would have loved her had she been as ordinary as she had pretended to be. She could give him the castle, of course, and supply the funding for a complete restoration. And what then? If he turned to her in gratitude, would she like that commitment any better?

No. It wouldn't work. She felt that truth right down to the core of her bruised but beating heart.

Trust. When the last vow was spoken, when the last argument settled, the bottom line was still that. Trust. Something she did with apparent foolishness. But she would never place her trust in anyone again—it hurt too much to be betrayed.

"Ah, a flower blooms in Lily's garden." Sebastian approached the pavilion with an expression both cautious and comforting. His dark hair flowed freely to his shoulders, and Monty longed to bury her hands in it, to pull those sensual lips to hers, to find comfort if only for a moment. But she just scooted over so that he could sit beside her on the broken step.

"They're gone," he said simply. "Your uncle made all the arrangements to take Eve's body back to the States. He talked at some length with the American ambassador this morning, but I don't know what was said."

"Aunt Jo?" Monty used the name as a question, wrapping her fingers together in a clasp of unforgiving strength. "Did she say anything to you?"

Seb shook his head. "She was very quiet, as was Sophie. Milton had a few choice words as he passed Charlotte in the great hall, but she quickly put him in his place."

"I dismissed the staff that Edwin brought from Paris. I've asked Charlotte and Louis to stay on and help catalog the missing items. I'm sure we'll never recover all the pieces, but perhaps there will be a few that can be used in the château's restoration."

"You're planning to restore the château?" Seb looked at her with surprise.

Her lips curved just shy of a smile. "No. You're planning to do that."

A frown etched into his forehead. "The gardens, yes. I had hoped to be allowed to finish those, but the rest...I don't think I'm qualified to oversee such a project. And the expense alone will be...well, prohibitive."

"I have lots of money, Sebastian. Didn't you know?"

Seb recognized the challenge. "Do you want me to lie, Monty?"

"No." She unclasped her hands, then clinched them again. "Let's have no more lies, Seb. Please, at least, be honest with me."

"Honest?" he repeated softly. "And will you believe me if I am? I am in love with you, Monty. I want to spend the rest of my life with you, marry you, be with you always, and yet even as I say the words, I know you will tell me that I'm lying."

"No. What I will tell you is that any feelings you do have for me are bound up in this place, in the long-ago actions of our great-grandparents, in the fact that you are the rightful heir to this castle on the Loire, not me."

"The château doesn't matter."

"Of course, it matters. You didn't come here to restore the gardens. You came to find a piece of your past. Maybe you are looking for a chalice, maybe that is all you really wanted. But, you see, if I stayed, if I allowed our relationship to continue, I'd never be sure, never know if it was really me you wanted. I'd always have to wonder if you would have loved me if I'd been someone like Eve, someone other than Montgomery Carlisle." She shook her head. "I won't settle for that uncertainty, Seb. Don't even ask me to."

She wouldn't meet his eyes, and he knew if he touched her now, she would get up and walk away. She was bruised, exhausted, unable to cope with any more emotion, unable to accept the idea that he might actually, truly love her. And he could do nothing to change her perceptions. Anger welled in his throat, but he didn't give it a voice. What could he say? He had offered her his heart and she had rejected it as unworthy.

"I am giving you the château," she continued in a voice as shallow as her breathing. "And I'll see that you have funds to restore it." She held up a hand to prevent any protest. "Please, don't be offended. The

Carlisles have stolen far too much from your family already. This is restitution, not a gift. Once the restoration is complete, you can give the château to the French ministry of culture, or you can keep it for your own, for your children and their children. The only thing I ask is that the tapestry of Joan of Arc remains in the bedroom where I stayed."

Her words, the casual giving of the château, was a slap to his face and Seb wanted to shake her, to rattle the composure that sealed off her heart like a glass coffin. She would *give* him the château, make restitution for the sins of the Carlisles. His jaw clenched with his anger, and without a word he pushed to his feet. With sheer willpower, he refused to wound her further by the outright rejection such a *gift* deserved. Instead, he gave her a stiff bow before he turned and walked away, taking with him his battered pride and a heartache so big it threatened to strangle him.

Monty watched him go, wishing she could call him back and love the hurt from his eyes. Or maybe she wanted to call him back to assuage the emptiness inside her. Either way, it didn't matter. She had placed her wealth between them, made him look it square in the eye and admit that it made a difference. Tears clumped in her throat and settled inside her in a cold and empty despair.

It was the eve of her twenty-seventh birthday and her innocence had died. The Carlisle curse had come true.

Chapter Twelve

Monty awakened with a start and sat up in bed, her heart racing, the blood pounding in her ears, her fingers clamped on the bed covers with a death grip. "Seb?" she whispered and half-expected him to materialize at the foot of her bed. But only an empty silence answered.

A long, deep sigh trembled past her lips and she made herself look deeper into the shadows, searching for anything out of the ordinary—as if anything at the château was ordinary. From the hidden door in the wall to the tapestry of Joan of Arc, the room was extraordinary. The whole château was a neglected but wondrous museum of France's rich history, and she knew a pang of disappointment that she could not take part in its resurrection.

On the floor by the outer door, four shadows marked her luggage, packed and ready for her early morning departure. She glanced at the travel alarm she'd set beside the bed. One minute after midnight. It was her birthday and she was going home. But where was home now that there was no one but her? Aunt Jo, Edwin, Sophie would all be gone from the house they had shared. The pretense that had been her family was shattered. And somehow she had survived.

Leaving the château, walking away with her pride, snuffing out the hope that Sebastian might have truly loved her. Those were the challenges she faced and must survive on this anniversary of her birth. Those were the battles she had yet to fight.

"Do they get any easier?" She turned the question to Joan in a whispered plea for advice. "Would you have fought a different fight, if you had known you weren't going to win?"

Monty couldn't see the tapestry in the dark, but she knew Joan was forever captured in her victories, not in her ultimate defeat. But was it defeat to believe? To trust in a future beyond the present? To attack the uncertainty of life with faith and courage?

Joan didn't answer, but someone did. Faraway, so indistinct Monty wasn't sure what she heard, there was a sound. A call. A stirring of spirits in the dark. And her name echoed through the night.

Montgomery Carlisle...

The hidden door panel swung slowly open and Monty caught a glimpse of candlelight, a single flame that beckoned with all the charisma of a siren's call. Without hesitation, and almost unaware of her actions, Monty got out of bed to follow. Spellbound by the impulse that urged her on, she slipped past the panel and into the darkness of the tunnel. The light cast an eerie glow as it moved steadily ahead, distant and out of reach but visible. Always visible.

Monty... Monty...

She heard the sound again as she moved forward quickly, unerringly, her bare feet sure and steady beneath her. Like a specter, she glided through the passageways, past the entrance that snaked into the north tower, following the faint but steady light that summoned her.

She didn't think of spiders or the uneven flooring beneath her bare feet. The chill didn't seep through the thin fabric of her nightshirt, although she knew it was there, all around her. She had no sense of time or place. The light ahead mesmerized her, claimed all her concentration and guided her toward a destiny she could not escape.

Monty...

At the bottom of a curving stairwell, she heard Seb call her name and wondered if it had been his voice she'd heard all along. The light moved up the stairs, disappearing around a turn, and although she had never been there before, Monty knew she was entering the south tower and climbing the path to the high turret above. But the south tower had been sealed. Hadn't Sebastian told her he had tried and failed to find the entrance? Hadn't she searched with him, trying to find some sign of a door?

But she was in the tower, feeling the smooth, worn rock face that had been built centuries before. Had

Edouard run his hands over the rocks as he climbed to the tower? Had he known he was going to jump to his death?

Monty...

For the first time since leaving her bed, Monty came fully alert. Seb was here, somewhere very near. He had climbed this stairway ahead of her. She sensed the lingering warmth of his touch on the rocks, felt it in the tips of her fingers, knew that he was waiting for her in the tower. The light shimmered, moving out of sight around the next twisting turn of the stairs. Monty hurried to follow, eager to find her lover, convinced that his heart had summoned her to this place, this time, and was giving her one last chance to find love.

But when she took the last step and entered the circular room at the top, he wasn't there. "Seb?" she whispered, but the sound echoed back to her, unanswered. The light had vanished and the chill suddenly was deep inside her. She rubbed her hands over her upper arms and couldn't remember what she was doing here or even how she'd gotten to this dark tower.

There were three windows cut into the room, all curved and narrow, and beyond them Monty saw only the glitter of a starry sky. Moving closer to the center window, she could make out the outline of rooftops in the village far below, saw in the distance the shimmer of moonlight on the river.

Monty...

The voice was louder here, and she was no longer certain that it was Sebastian who called her.

Monty...

Turning slowly, inexplicably drawn toward the sound, she faced the window and saw a wisp of movement, like breath condensing in cold weather. Monty blinked to clear her vision, but all she could see was the many-faceted roofline of the château through the far window. Against all her instincts of self-preservation, she crossed the tower room and ran her hand over the smooth cobbled surface of the windowsill. Instantly, she saw an image in her mind's eye, knew that if she were to look out and straight down from the window, she would see the path Edouard had taken to his death on the broken battlements below. She could feel the long-ago echoes of his pain, as if he had jumped from the window only moments before she entered.

With a shudder, Monty took a step back. The window was so small, though, hardly big enough for a man to fit through. Seb, certainly, was too large. She wasn't even sure she was small enough to wiggle her way through. Moving closer again, she ran her hand along the rock framework, putting her shoulders against the opening, looking for an explanation. Beyond the window, the turrets of the château formed a dark and jagged line, framed in moonlight, half-hidden in midnight shadows.

And then she saw it. Like a diamond catching the sun, it caught her eye. The chalice. Nestled in the crook of the rooftop, sheltered by a slight overhang and hidden from view except from this one particular vantage point, just an arm's length from where she stood. The de Vergille chalice. Seb's Holy Grail. It was real. It was here. He hadn't lied to her, after all.

Monty leaned out, stretching, reaching for the treasure that was just beyond her grasp. She wedged her hips in the narrow window frame and with legs securely touching the tower floor, she maneuvered her upper body through the opening.

Success. Her fingers touched the cool, slick feel of silver. Another quarter of an inch and she'd have hold of it. Seb would be so happy when she showed him this one small piece of his past. She sucked in her breath and wiggled her hips, giving her fingers the extra elevation needed to grasp the handle.

With a tug, the chalice came free and Monty's feet left the floor. With a sickening thump, she slid precariously forward and hung high above the ground, balanced like a tightrope walker without a net. Instinctively, she tucked the chalice close to her chest and looked for a lifeline. She realized very quickly that there was nothing.... No flagpole, no roofing tile, no overhang close enough to grab hold of. She was bent like a sausage, her stomach scraping the outer ledge while her knees pressed against the inside ledge and provided her only means of balance. With a wiggle of her hips, she realized that any movement was going to propel her forward into eternity, not backward into safety.

Her heart tapped out an SOS as her brain spiraled out a string of random and totally useless information. Did fire trucks have ladders that extended far enough to reach her? Who would hear her call for help, anyway? Aunt Jo had been wrong. Monty was going to die on her birthday. Not on the day before. What was she doing here and why, oh, why couldn't she have pricked her finger on a spindle as Sleeping Beauty had? Sleeping for a hundred years, waiting for Prince Charming's kiss to awaken her, suddenly didn't seem like such a bad deal.

"Monty!"

She thought at first his voice was just another hallucination, but then she felt his fingers bite into her ankle and the relief shot through her with such riotous warmth that she slipped forward. Sebastian grabbed for her other ankle, found a firm grip and began rocking her slowly, easing her back into the room, away from danger. "Wiggle your hips," Seb called. "This is a tight fit."

As if she hadn't noticed. She moved cautiously backward, wiggling, rocking, until her toes touched the floor and Seb's helping hands found a new position on either hip. Her elbow bumped the outside of the tower and Monty realized she had another problem. "I've got the chalice," she said over her shoulder. "I found it out here on the roof. It's real, Seb. I'm holding it in my hands."

"Drop it," he commanded.

"Don't be ridiculous. This is the Holy Grail. It belongs to your family, to you...."

"Monty, drop the chalice. Let it go."

"But it will be irreparably damaged if I drop it."

He cursed in French. "*You* will be irreparably damaged if you don't drop it. Monty, please. I love you. I could not go on living if you were to die."

Maybe he would have said the same thing to any damsel in distress, but Monty decided he was right. A silver chalice wasn't worth the risk. With a sigh of regret, she tossed it up, hoping it might find the way back to its hiding place. But the chalice spun high overhead, a silver fish against a black sea, and began a slow spiral downward, turning and spilling its contents into the night air. Monty watched in astonishment as a shower of sparkling red caught and splintered the rays of moonlight, then sifted over her like sharp-edged dew. She opened her hands and caught a dewdrop in her palm just as Sebastian pulled her back through the window and into the tower room.

His arms closed tight around her, and she felt him tremble as his lips ravaged hers in a devastating kiss. Their bodies had but one accord and they sank together to the floor, still holding, still kissing, still clinging to one another.

"*Mon amour. Mon amour. Je ne peux pas vivre sans toi. Je t'adore.*" He pressed her head against his chest and held her for endless precious moments. "Why do you take such foolish chances? If you had fallen..." His voice broke and the erratic, frightened beat of his heart took over the protest. "If I hadn't awakened suddenly and thought I heard you call to me, I might not have been here to save you. I don't know how you unlocked the tower door, but when I saw it was open and heard the empty silence in the room above... I have never known such fear. Please, Monty, I do not wish to live without you.''

By the tension in his arms, the tightness of his hold on her, Monty thought he must mean what he said. She might have responded that she didn't want to live without him, either, but her head was buried against his chest, making talking difficult. And there was something strange and magical about the night that surrounded them. Something that kept her quiet, compelled her to listen, implored her to believe the words he said. She ran her closed fists over his shoulders, holding him as he was holding her.

"You must believe me. I don't care what name you go by. You can be Montgomery Carlisle or Joan of Arc. I don't care about the château. I don't care if you give away every penny of the Carlisle fortune. I love you, Monty. I want to spend my life proving that to you. Let me show you. Let me sign something, an agreement that I will claim nothing that belongs to you."

Slowly, Monty drew away from the embrace. Slowly, she looked for the truth in his eyes and found it. "I love you, Sebastian. Forgive me for being so insecure. Forgive me for not trusting you. Forgive me for nearly selling out our future for something so pathetically empty as money."

He lifted her hand to his lips. "There is nothing to forgive. Not if you will marry me."

"Yes," she said. "I will, but there is one stipulation."

"Name it."

"Well, you see, there's a ring in the infamous Carlisle collection. And this particular ring comes with magical powers...the wearer must be true to his love, forever."

"That, Mademoiselle Carlisle, will not be a problem. Is there a magical ring for you, as well?"

She smiled into his dark and seductive eyes. "I'll have one made from the Carlisle Ruby. It once belonged to Joan of Arc."

"Indeed." Seb turned her hand over and began to kiss each fingertip in turn. She opened her palm for his caress.

"What is this?"

In her palm lay a single bloodred ruby. It caught and reflected the candlelight, becoming a glowing ember in her hand. She stared at the ruby in confusion. "When I let go of the chalice, these flew out. A whole shower of them. A fortune in jewels. You're rich, Sebastian. Well, at least you will be if we can find them again."

He seemed mesmerized by the gleaming gem. "Lily's rubies," he said. "I didn't believe they existed," he said. "I thought the stories were a myth. And yet, something beyond my reason compelled me to search for them despite my doubts."

"Lily's rubies," Monty whispered. "Her blood turned to rubies in Edouard's hands. But I don't understand...?" The air in the tower pulsed with a dual heartbeat, a loud, rhythmic, steady cadence. Monty felt a burning sensation in her palm, coughed as the smell of thick black smoke reached her nostrils, and suddenly sensed the spinning, whirling, shifting of another dimension all around her.

The tower room glowed with a light as sharp and brilliant as a diamond. Warmth invaded Monty, tingling through her in a thousand bursts of energy. And then it spiraled upward in a single shattering sensation and was gone. She looked at Seb, only to find him staring out the far window at a strange and ghostly light. He took her hand and together they stood and walked to the window.

Below in the garden a fire blazed, red and gold and white. The maze was burning. All of it at once. The flames consumed it in a matter of seconds, and then the fire went out—as if it had never been—leaving nothing but the broken pavilion, touching not another shrub in the garden.

"Lily is free," Seb whispered as his arms circled Monty and pulled her back against his chest. "Her spirit and Edouard's have been freed by our love."

Monty listened to the steady rhythm of his heartbeat as she watched a plume of feathery smoke drift upward and away.

"Sebastian?"

"My love?"

"Today is my birthday."

He turned her in his arms and caressed her with his eyes. "I will have to find a present for you."

She shook her head. "You are the only gift I want . . . today and for the rest of my life."

He dipped his head in an obedient bow. "Your wish is granted, my princess. Now and forever more."

COMING NEXT MONTH

#553 THE MARRYING TYPE by Judith Arnold

Like his friends, Steve Chambliss vowed to be a bachelor forever. Then he appeared on "The Gwen Talbot Show"—and fell hard for the hostess herself. She didn't mix business with pleasure, and confirmed bachelors didn't mix lust with love...or did they? *Don't miss the first book in the Studs series!*

#554 THE INVISIBLE GROOM by Barbara Bretton
More Than Men

Saying "I do" might be the hardest thing Chase Quinn ever had to do—but it was the only way he'd be free of the curse that rendered him invisible. Only thing was, the see-through playboy had to *mean* it!

#555 FINDING DADDY by Judy Christenberry

Kelly Abbott needed a baby—she didn't need or want the man who came along with it. Trouble was, the only guy who met all her requirements—James Townsend—had designs on being a full-time hubby and daddy!

#556 LOVE POTION #5 by Cathy Gillen Thacker

As far as Remy Beauregard was concerned, Jill Sutherland was nothing more than a Yankee career woman with too much attitude—until he accidentally drank a love potion. With every gulp, Jill looked better...until Remy found himself agreeing to a steamy bayou trek. Unfortunately, the antidote Jill sought was now the last thing on Remy's mind.

AVAILABLE THIS MONTH:

#549 THE WEDDING GAMBLE
Muriel Jensen

#550 SEDUCING SPENCER
Nikki Rivers

#551 CRUISIN' MR. DIAMOND
Lynn Leslie

#552 THE PAUPER AND THE PRINCESS
Karen Toller Whittenburg

1994 MISTLETOE MARRIAGES
HISTORICAL CHRISTMAS STORIES

With a twinkle of lights and a flurry of snowflakes, Harlequin Historicals presents *Mistletoe Marriages,* a collection of four of the most magical stories by your favorite historical authors. The perfect way to celebrate the season!

Brimming with romance and good cheer, these heartwarming stories will be available in November wherever Harlequin books are sold.

RENDEZVOUS by Elaine Barbieri
THE WOLF AND THE LAMB by Kathleen Eagle
CHRISTMAS IN THE VALLEY by Margaret Moore
KEEPING CHRISTMAS by Patricia Gardner Evans

Add a touch of romance to your holiday with *Mistletoe Marriages* Christmas Stories!

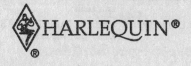

HARLEQUIN®

MMXS94

AMERICAN ◆ ROMANCE®

You asked for it...you've got it. More MEN!

We're thrilled to bring you another special edition of the popular
MORE THAN MEN series.

Like those who have come before him, Chase Quinn is more than tall,
dark and handsome. All of these men have extraordinary powers that
make them "more than men." But whether they are able to grant you
three wishes or live forever, make no mistake—their greatest, most
extraordinary power is of seduction.

So make a date in October with Chase Quinn in

#554 THE INVISIBLE GROOM
by Barbara Bretton

This summer, come cruising with Harlequin Books!

PORTS
OF CALL

In July, August and September, excitement, danger and, of course, romance can be found in Lynn Leslie's exciting new miniseries PORTS OF CALL. Not only can you cruise the South Pacific, the Caribbean and the Nile, your journey will also take you to Harlequin Superromance®, Harlequin Intrigue® and Harlequin American Romance®.

- In July, cruise the South Pacific with SINGAPORE FLING, a Harlequin Superromance
- NIGHT OF THE NILE from Harlequin Intrigue will heat up your August
- September is the perfect month for CRUISIN' MR. DIAMOND from Harlequin American Romance

So, cruise through the summer with LYNN LESLIE and HARLEQUIN BOOKS!

CRUISE

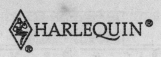

HARLEQUIN®

Weddings, Inc.

THE VENGEFUL GROOM
Sara Wood

Legend has it that those married in Eternity's chapel are destined for a lifetime of happiness. But happiness isn't what Giovanni wants from marriage—it's revenge!

Ten years ago, Tina's testimony sent Gio to prison—for a crime he didn't commit. *Now* he's back in Eternity and looking for a bride. *Now* Tina is about to learn just how ruthless and disturbingly sensual Gio's brand of vengeance can be.

THE VENGEFUL GROOM, available in October from Harlequin Presents, is the fifth book in Harlequin's new cross-line series, **WEDDINGS, INC.** Be sure to look for the sixth book, **EDGE OF ETERNITY,** by Jasmine Cresswell (Harlequin Intrigue #298), coming in November.

WED5

HARLEQUIN® AMERICAN ROMANCE®

Four sexy hunks who vowed they'd never take "the vow" of marriage...

What happens to this Bachelor Club when, one by one, they find the right bachelorette?

Meet four of the most perfect men:

Steve: **THE MARRYING TYPE**
Judith Arnold
(October)

Tripp: **ONCE UPON A HONEYMOON**
Julie Kistler
(November)

Ukiah: **HE'S A REBEL**
Linda Randall Wisdom
(December)

Deke: **THE WORLD'S LAST BACHELOR**
Pamela Browning
(January)